Perpetual Locomotion

Paul McKnight

Acknowledgements

Thanks to Alan Fleming for his cover painting, and for his patience in dealing with my revisions.

Thanks to all the people who read Guilt Edged and took the trouble to tell me that they'd enjoyed it. I'd like to invite all of them round for dinner, but we don't have anywhere near enough cutlery.

And thanks to my wife, Pam, who was quite happy to proof-read the story, until she came to the crowded railway station platform scene. She doesn't like crowds.

Dee Robinson, once again, supplied the author's photograph.

Preface: The Non-Fiction Bit

The Chinnor to Princes Risborough Railway is situated in South Oxfordshire and Buckinghamshire and runs along almost five miles of track at the base of the picturesque Chiltern Hills. The line was originally opened in the mid-nineteenth century and was hardly a great commercial success, partly due to the failure to link up the towns of Watlington and Wallingford. Passenger services finally ceased in 1957.

Thanks to the efforts of the CPRR Association, the railway started to come back to life in 1989 and is now a very popular tourist attraction, with its steam and classic diesel locomotives. It makes far more money now than it ever did in its early service life.

It is beyond doubt that the events described in this book have never happened, nor will ever happen.

Well I hope not…..

Contents

Prologue

The two young men lay, soaking wet and breathless, on the river bank just to the west of Oxford's Magdalen Bridge. One of their friends was trying to steer a punt towards the bank, the unwieldy craft and his inexperience making it hard work. Other people were attempting to reach them from the hire company's office, just the other side of the bridge.

"Speak to me, mate." One of the young men manages to prop himself up on his elbow, while his companion is still coughing and spluttering and spitting out the river water he'd ingested. "I thought you were a goner there."

"You saved my life."

"That's a great comeback line. Thanks. You'll be okay. Everything's alright now."

Soon, the latecomers to the rescue party are clustering round, offering the next stage of practical help. The siren of an ambulance could be heard, getting louder as it cut through the lunchtime traffic. The university couldn't afford to lose this particular student.

"But that's what you get for showing off." They grinned at each other, now the danger was past.

These two had become acquainted during these first months at Oxford University, but the Asian kid could be quite difficult, a bit arrogant, and inclined to want to display his talents, whether he really had them or not. Hence the falling from the back of the punt and getting himself wedged underneath it, long enough to take in more water than was good for him.

"Glad you were there, my friend. I live to fight another day."

Not At Her Best First Thing

"Are you sitting comfortably?"

The occupant of the chair, when conscious, usually considered herself to be Mrs Melanie Rainham, but she hadn't been conscious or self aware for a very long time. She hardly stirred, and so the sarcasm the questioner had intended was wasted. Instead of repeating the question, he kicked one of the chair legs in front of him with a steel toe-capped engineer's boot. Finally, she began to show some reaction to the noise and movement; a low groan and a flickering of eyelids. She hadn't made any noise herself since she'd lapsed from screaming in terror into unconsciousness some time ago. About four years ago, give or take a few weeks.

Although not exactly aware of her surroundings, she was coming to the realisation that she was awake. Awake, with absolutely no idea of where she was or why she was there, her eyes opened wide in panic and her arms and legs fought against the bonds that held her to the chair. Not unreasonably, she reverted to screaming in terror and frustration, and then screamed again when she was able to focus on the character standing in front of her. Apart from the boots, he wore a blue bib and brace overall, a checked shirt and a peaked cap and, on a wrinkly old face, a big smile that an independent observer might have considered to be in poor taste, considering the woman's obvious distress. And he was thinking that this was shaping up to be the worst case of getting out of the wrong side of the bed ever.

The question came again, also, frankly, in poor taste.

"Are you sitting comfortably? Then I'll begin. I've always wanted to say that. But never mind all that. Like the Proverb says; a little sleep, a little slumbering, a little folding of the hands and we'll all be up the swanee. So, time to get up. I need you to give me a hand with something. Do you like rail travel?"

"You sadistic bastard! What kind of warped mind have you got?"

"I would say that's a bit rich coming from you. Last time you were out and about I had to stop you from setting fire to a house with a young mum and two kids."

"You're that bloody demon, aren't you? Mister E."

He clucked both of his tongues reproachfully.

"That's not my name, as well you know, and I'll thank you very much not to use it."

The memory starts to filter back into Melanie's mind; a jumble of memories really. That last time, yes, her last memory. A can of petrol in her hand. And so angry. Did she really intend to…..? Becoming gradually more lucid, she recalled how her cousin Yvonne had died of a drug and drink overdose and how she'd enlisted the help of a vengeance demon, who came highly recommended by the way, to punish the man who should have prevented the tragedy, and how she'd waited twenty seven years for the demon to get the job done, only for said demon to, in her opinion, fall short of providing a quality service. No wonder she'd taken the law into her own hands. If you want a job done properly, let a woman do it, was her view. And now this! She was being punished for going against the demon's plan. Who's the bloody client here anyway?

What was, again, in her opinion, justifiable righteous indignation, wasn't enough to prevent her collapsing into a fit of sobbing as a whole crowd of emotions flooded in on her. Remorse was in there too, but did she deserve this? The demon stood patiently and silently, to give her time to process her thoughts and feelings. He could have read her mind if he chose to do so, but it didn't take a mind-reader to know that her first question would be about her husband and her two children. Through the clearing mental and emotional fog, she remembered that she was a wife and mother, or she had been. A wife, a mother, an arsonist.

"Where's Greg? And the kids? Do they know where I am?"

"I'll come to that soon….."

"I need to know now!"

"I said soon! Now, if I let you out of that chair, don't do anything stupid."

"Like what?"

"Well, look at me. I'm a little old man in a bib and brace overall. I know! It's the wrong size; makes me look even smaller. You might feel justified in giving me a good thrashing, but just remember what happened the first time we met, eh?"

"Are you threatening me?" Her bravado didn't block out what he'd reminded her of, their first encounter in her friend's library back in 1991. Melanie had had the temerity to challenge his credentials (he hadn't looked very demonic then either) and the result was that a character that she thought looked like a wizened old retired accountant who'd fallen on hard times and come for a job as a gardener, suddenly turned into something like the Incredible Hulk's big brother.

"Threatening? No, not exactly. I just don't want you to waste your energy. As I've already said, I want you to do something for me."

"Do something for you? I'm not doing anything for you, you bastard. You tie me to a chair and leave me in this grotty room and you want me to help you. Fuck off!"

"Well it's up to you. Either you do what I ask or you can stay in that chair forever. It doesn't bother me. And I have to say that I don't approve of all the swearing. Please curb your tongue."

"Fuck you!"

That's all she manages to say, because her lips are instantly replaced by a substantial zip fastener.

"That's better. Now, nod if you're finally listening."

The wide eyed and shaking Melanie does so and the demon reaches for the straps holding her to the chair. He pauses before untying them:

"Nothing stupid. Promise?"

She nods again.

"And no gutter language?"

Her glare conveys some pretty harsh thoughts, which he fortunately, once more, chooses not to read, but she nods again and the demon completes the task of freeing her. He stands back as if to admire his work. He's done a perfect job of restoring her lips. Melanie rubs her wrists and ankles where her recent struggling has chaffed them, and then looks up at her captor.

"What are you grinning at, you….I mean what's so funny?"

"Nothing's funny. It's just good to see you looking so well after all this time."

"After all this time? How long have I been sitting here?"

"Remember you promised not to swear?"

"How long?"

"Four years, give or take a few weeks….. Oh, now, come on!..... Do your promises mean nothing?"

Distractions

The cyclist was distracted, and not just today. He seemed to be permanently distracted, preoccupied, unable to find peace of mind. Ever since his wife mysteriously disappeared about a year before, in the Spring of 2018. There was no explanation, no note, nothing to suggest that anything was wrong with her or with their marriage. She had simply vanished and so had her car. Motorway cameras had spotted it travelling north-west and there was CCTV evidence that she had been in the outskirts of Birmingham. And why were the police looking at that? Because they were investigating a couple of arson attacks and wanted to "eliminate her from their inquiries". The idea of his wife being an arsonist was beyond ridiculous, as far as he was concerned. She was a loving wife and mother, not a bloody terrorist, for Christ's sake. Surely it was a coincidence that the properties that had burned belonged to their friends, Chris and Trisha. You don't set fire to your friends' stuff, do you, their house, their shop? Since then, a distinct coolness had developed between him and them, even though they said, not very convincingly he thought, that they agreed with him. The friendship wasn't standing the test of time and tribulation, for some reason. Stuff 'em. It was taking all his time to keep his head together and to be a single parent to his distraught son and daughter. And everywhere he went, he kept looking for his wife, kept thinking he'd seen her in a crowd.

Today was one of those days. He was cycling through Oxford, heading for the rugby club on Iffley Road where he was trying to get back into coaching a junior team, something he'd been doing on a voluntary basis once his own playing days were over. As he approached The Plain Roundabout, he spotted somebody walking out of a shop; a woman in a green coat, tall and blond. It could be her! What he didn't spot as he hesitated was the tipper truck that came up alongside him, bound for the left lane towards Headington, as he started to move across to the right hand filter for Iffley Road.

It could have been worse. The truck's rear wheel propelled him at speed into a parked delivery van. It could have been better if he'd been wearing a helmet. He was taken to hospital with what the media described as life-changing injuries. The lorry driver was arrested at the scene and subsequently charged with a number of motoring offences. The observations of eye-witnesses who testified that the cyclist had been meandering before the collision saved him from a conviction for dangerous driving, but the charges for drug-driving and the driving without any of the relevant documents to his name stuck. Cyclists' groups called for more to be done to protect two wheeled road users, but none of this, or the efforts of the country's best medical staff would help the cyclist walk again.

Incentive Scheming

"Four years! Tell me you're joking! That's impossible."

The demon shakes his head and rolls his purple tinged eyes in exasperation. Perhaps he needed a different persona. Nobody took the little old man seriously. Well not at first.

"Surely you know me better than that. How many times do I have to demonstrate what is or isn't possible? You've been sitting there for four years. You'll be complaining next that it's not a comfy chair."

"It wasn't anything. I didn't feel anything. How is that possible?"

"I've had you on life-support, but without all the wires and tubes and drips and those machines that go beep every time your heart beats. Easy. I may go as far as to add peasy."

Melanie had asked the question, but she's not really listening to the answer because, once again she's overwhelmed with the realisation that she has no idea where her husband and children are, or if they know where she is. And, oh dear God! If this evil bastard standing in front of her is telling the truth when he says four years.......

"Where's my family? I need to see them. They'll be going frantic with worry."

"They were indeed going frantic with worry, for quite a long while after you disappeared, actually. It's more a sort of collective resignation now. They still can't believe you're gone, but they've learned to live with it. I did hear that they were thinking of holding a memorial service."

"What!? They think I'm dead?"

"Of course they think you're dead. What would you conclude if somebody went missing for four years? They can't think of a reason why you would run away, so they've speculated about abduction and murder or you being swept away in a river. Then there's the slave trade of course; quite a market for tall, white blondes in some places.... What?"

"You sick, heartless bastard. And never mind looking all disapproving at my language. This is all because I broke your made up rules, isn't it? I overstepped your mark. How long were you planning to leave me here if you didn't want me to do something for you? And there's fat chance of that, by the way!"

"I could leave you there for as long as I like. Forever, if necessary. And as regards your cooperation; either you do, or you go back in the chair. I can probably find somebody else. Your daughter, Emma, for example. She'd probably jump at the chance."

Melanie had subsided into near-silent sobs, but at the mention of her daughter's name she sat bolt upright.

"What's Emma got to do with this, for God's sake? You haven't got her somewhere as well, have you? I don't care who you are, if you've hurt my family…."

Heedless of the consequences, she stands up and hurls herself at the demon, who, mercifully, merely grabs her flailing arms and restrains her.

"Just calm down!"

Human males have mostly learned, often the hard way, the folly of telling human females to calm down, but there was clearly at least one gap in this non-human's education. The stream of abuse that proceeded from Melanie's mouth soon put him right. He wisely decided to let it go, this time; she was having a bad morning, to be fair.

"There's absolutely nothing wrong with your daughter. She's at home, perfectly well. But there is something I need to tell you, and it may make you more inclined to help me. I warn you, though, it's not all good news."

He guides her back into the chair and she sits there in stunned silence, waiting for the next bombshell.

"Emma's fine, and so is your son, Alex. But about three years ago your husband had an accident. He was knocked off his bicycle and, no, no; he's not dead, but he was badly injured. He's in a wheelchair now."

"Oh no…" The tears start rolling down her cheeks. "You have to let me go back. You can't keep me here! It's not fair…"

"Of course it's not fair. Human life is frequently not fair, but it's not my place, nor my inclination, to go round cheering everybody up, making everything fair. I was, after all, a vengeance demon when you met me. In fact, that's why you met me, isn't it? Nothing's changed."

"Don't you think I've suffered enough? That bastard that let my cousin die, you let him off the hook."

"I did eventually, yes. Besides, he was doing a good enough job of beating himself up anyway. But let me remind you of something about your precious cousin Yvonne, and before you say anything, I have never entertained any qualms about speaking ill of the dead. Some of them have been very rude about me too. She'd fooled her lover with a faked suicide stunt once already, so when she did it again, he decided to call her bluff. Turned out to be a poor choice, I concede, but you can at least see his point of view."

"I don't have to see anything of the sort. He still let her die."

"As you wish. But you found all that out, didn't you? The cousin who cried wolf."

"Okay, yes! I did. But she still didn't deserve to die!"

"I don't know. She was a very foolish woman in my opinion. And I notice that you're all concerned about your own family, but what fate did you have in store for that young family that you were pursuing with a gallon of petrol, eh? Tell me that. Did you even think about the consequences? So I'll let you off the hook when I'm good and ready and not before."

"Isn't four years in a chair long enough?"

"As I said, when I'm ready. And I've been very busy for the last four years."

"That again! Always busy. Last time it took me twenty seven years to get any service."

"And it might have been another twenty seven if it hadn't been for your daughter."

"What on earth do you mean? Have you told her where I am?"

"Look, you've just woken up. You're a bit grouchy, putting it mildly. You must be hungry or at least in need of a cappuccino or something. I think I could do with a pot of tea myself. What day is it? Tuesday? They do special discounts for pensioners on Tuesdays. Shall we go and chase up a bit of nourishment? Then I'll explain why I want your help."

Troll in a Hole

Gerald English was back on Facebook. He'd joined another group that, so far, hadn't got round to kicking him off for his own interpretation of the concept of freedom of speech, which was merely unalloyed bigotry. His feelings regarding the hoity-toity middle classes who were spoiling the local pubs for working men were freely expressed, those very same stuck-up out-of-towners who pushed property prices beyond the reach of local people.

He was running out of aliases; Anglo Gerry had been rumbled by the Benson group admin. He was thinking of a new fake profile as Giuseppe Inglesi. The thought of falling back on a bit of polite restraint had never entered his head for a second. So this time it was the Great Afferton Village Noticeboard which found itself the lucky recipient of his views.

The particular thread of conversation he was looking at now wasn't one he'd started, but it was on a topic he liked to air his opinions about; Bloody cyclists! The author of the post had merely commented how difficult it was to overtake large groups of cyclists who were out training on Sunday mornings. These were the particular lycra-clad twats that got Gerald going. In fact it was for using just that unsavoury expression that he'd been blocked from another Facebook community.

Regardless of whether his opinion of cyclists could be justified, he could have followed their lead and partaken in some form of physical activity to keep his weight down, although he'd already arrived at that point in life where he would be advised to consult his doctor before starting anything strenuous. He was, however, inordinately proud of his thick, dark hair; hardly a grey one anywhere. He liked to remain clean-shaven, his face being where the grey ones sprouted. Gerald thought that if he managed to hold his belly in as often as he could, he looked rather impressive, but he shied away from canvassing other views on that one.

And so the Facebook post descended into a barrage of comments about how cyclists don't pay road tax and they should be insured if they were going to use the roads that motorists paid for. Somebody had the temerity to suggest that a lot of cyclists are insured and asked how you could tell whether motorists were insured and nobody seemed to have a good answer to that one, but that was soon lost in the theme of cyclists being arrogant and up on the moral high ground.

A new contributor calling herself Krazy Karen suggested chucking curry at them from the car's passenger window when you eventually managed to get past; it's what she and her friends used to do. That amused Gerald. Future plan there. He remembered the time when he'd wound down his car window and shouted a four letter expletive at a cyclist; not the "f" word that practically everybody seems to use, but the more anatomical one that polite ladies don't like to hear. Not his proudest moment. Then again, maybe it was; he wasn't a high achiever.

He contributed the comment that cyclists who dither about all over the road, getting in the way of drivers and then complain when they get hurt, have only themselves to blame.

Somebody called Emma said that was a terrible thing to say. Her father had been knocked off his bike by a truck and was now paralysed from the waist down.

True to form, Gerald didn't hesitate: "Well he should of looked where he was going then."

And then, one second he was behind a keyboard, hammering out bad grammar, the next he found himself riding a very cumbersome cargo bike. These things are hard enough to ride at the best of times, but this one's front basket was piled high with vegetables, mainly potatoes, and having to pedal in too high a gear, weaving round the potholes on a busy main road was making him feel very hot under the collar. Looking down to see if the wretched machine even had a gear changer did nothing for the overall stability. Gerald hated bikes.

Coffee and Consequences

Melanie was in a downward spiral of grief, anger, confusion and the frustration of not getting answers to her innumerable questions at the speed she would have liked. This demon was insufferably stubborn about controlling information. But she had to admit he was right about one thing. She could do with a cup of coffee. And something to eat. She had no idea how she'd been kept alive for the last four years, and she didn't think she wanted to know either, but four years was a long time to go between proper meals.

"Come on! The place is just round the corner and they'll still be doing breakfast and….oh damn. It's not Tuesday. It's Friday. Full price!"

She followed him out of the dingy little room and then realised she needed the facilities in an even smaller room. Four years is a long time without a comfort break too.

"Hang on a minute."

Melanie rejoined the demon at the bottom of the stairs and he led the way out onto the street. It felt good to be in fresh air again. A bit too bright though. The demon noticed her squinting and dimmed the sky a couple of notches. The air wasn't completely fresh, but the aroma of coffee and cooking bacon didn't spoil it one bit. The coffee shop was on the corner of the next terraced street and the bell over the door jingled as they let themselves in.

"Morning Charlie!"

"Morning Derek. The usual?"

"The usual, Charlie. And a cappuccino for my friend here while she peruses your menu."

Melanie elected to perch on a stool at the bar just inside the window; she'd been sitting in an allegedly comfortable chair for way too long. The demon joined her, struggling to hitch his small frame onto the adjacent stool, while Charlie busied himself preparing their drinks.

"I know what you're thinking," the demon said quietly.

"Of course you do, but I'm going to say it anyway. Derek? Really?"

"Awful, isn't it? But I'm a regular here. I had to tell him something, didn't I? My real name would be extremely hard to pronounce, even by Xhosa standards."

"I couldn't care less what you're called actually, but don't ever introduce me as your friend again. We're not friends. I can't think of any word that's far enough away from 'friend' to describe how I feel about you right now."

"I didn't wake you up to be my friend. I woke you up because I require your assistance. Although I do hate it when there's what you might call a bit of an atmosphere, don't you?"

Melanie just stared at him with a mix of scorn and disbelief. This sadistic monster professed a sensitive side.

"So why me and why now? And before you answer that, I'll have a Full English with wholemeal toast. Please," she added as an afterthought, in case he picked her up on her bad manners as well as her swearing.

"And another thing; why are you wearing a boiler suit, or whatever you call it, that's too big for you? And the cap's ridiculous. Are you trying to look young and trendy, or something?"

"Dearie me! Are you always this irritable when you need feeding? Charlie, quick as you like with that food. This female's getting hangry!"

He turns back to face Melanie, and feigns looking offended. Melanie doesn't feign:

"This female?"

"Sorry. Aren't you? I'm sorry you don't approve of my attire, but it's all part of my new interest. You'd call it a hobby I suppose."

"You have time for a hobby? I thought you were always busy. And last time we met, I seem to remember you were into religion."

"Ah yes. Well not religion as such, but I did find the Bible quite interesting from an 'understand the other side' point of view. I have to say, if you think I'm cruel, you should take a look at the so-called good guys. Unbelievable. But there's a lot of good one-liners in there. There's a time for everything under the sun, for example, and I see it's time for your breakfast and then, as you almost politely requested, I'll take the time to answer your questions."

Melanie takes her plate and cutlery and, just as in happier times, devours the mushrooms first. How can fungus taste so good?

"That's interesting. You enjoy eating something that grows out of decay. Reminds me of home."

"That's disgusting."

"So is talking with your mouth full. So you eat, and I'll talk. Why you and why now? you said."

Melanie swallows a bit of sausage to give her the right to interrupt.

"Yes, and what has my daughter got to do with this? How have you got her involved?"

"Ah, well she contacted me."

Brushing off the volley of baked beans which neither of them had been expecting, he continued.

"You remember when you first contacted me, through our late, lamented friend, Joyce? Yes? She requested my presence by using an incantation in one of her ancient spell books, a book which I understand she bequeathed to you. With me so far? Just nod….Good! We come, then, to your daughter Emma, who had reached the point of going through your belongings, trying to see what she could give to the local charity shop. As you know, she's into recycling and what have you. And, unusually for a young person, decluttering."

"Oh great! She's been giving my stuff away!"

"Well they'd all come to the conclusion that you were dead, obviously. But this one book looked really special and of course Joyce's bookmark was still in the chapter 'Summon Ye A Vengeance Demon'.

"She didn't!"

"She did! Her life had become very stressful. You weren't there of course, and her dad had become unfortunately incapacitated, as I mentioned earlier. Her university career had been shelved so that she could look after him."

Melanie suddenly found she'd lost her appetite.

"What about my son? Alex?"

"Drinks a lot. Very argumentative. Very angry. And neither of them think that the truck driver who knocked their father off his bike was sufficiently punished by the law, or was particularly repentant. And he continued driving without the necessary documents. So your daughter felt she had good cause to get revenge. I don't think she really believed the incantation would work, judging by the look on her face when she came out from behind the sofa."

"You didn't do the big transformation thing, did you?"

"Not at all. She wasn't as sceptical as you, to her credit. But she's really got it in for that lorry driver."

"I'd like to get my hands on him myself!"

"Well I think you may have that opportunity if you decide to cooperate with my plan. Ah! Now you're interested."

"Of course I'm interested. I'm still sceptical though. For one thing, that you'd actually come back to help me, especially with you being so busy all the time."

"Your cynicism is noted. But it's not altruism. That's not me at all. No. It's just that, when somebody invokes that spell I have no choice but to drop whatever I'm doing and respond. Professional rules, you see."

"Professional! Huh!"

"I know you aren't impressed, but I could show you some five star reviews on Faustpilot.com if you like. No? Anyway, I'm not here to help you directly. You're here to help me and, of course, I'm under contract to your daughter. But this time I have a scheme to mix business with pleasure; my pleasure that is, not yours."

"No surprise there. But if you can keep me alive for four years, you seem to bloody well know everything and you even have a dimmer switch for the sky, how could you possibly need my help?"

"I've always wanted to be an engine driver. You're going to be a trolley dolly."

Message For You, Mo

Maureen had to stand in line and wait for the customer in front to pay for his purchases. "B.L.Z(ee). Bubb's Emporium of Magic" was unusually busy.

Mr Bubb, as he called himself for trading purposes, was speaking to the customer, who was a balding, middle-aged man with a Star Wars sweatshirt.

"So they should be in stock the day after tomorrow. If I'm not here just show your receipt and tell them you have one reserved."

"What was all that about?" Maureen asks when the customer has left.

"Hello Mo. Good to see you again. That was about these cuddly Satans we've bought in. People can't get enough of them. But here's the laugh; that is, if your sense of humour is extremely elastic. I pretend I haven't got any in stock so the punters can tell their friends that B.L.Z(ee). Bubb has a devil put aside for them. Pathetic, I know, but it shifts the stock."

"Good grief! Could be worse; they could ask you if you can do the fandango. Stupidest question I ever heard."

"Worse than 'Should I stay or should I go'?"

"Much. Now look Bert, I didn't come here to talk about song lyrics. Have you got anything for me? I'm a busy woman."

"No you're not. You're neither busy, nor a woman."

"Shush! It's the best disguise yet; a dowdy looking fifty something with flat shoes and a carrier bag. Nobody pays me any attention. I might as well be invisible."

"Why don't you just do that then? Be invisible."

"Because I've just rented a nice little flat in town. I like to sit there with a glass of red wine of an evening, have a friend round perhaps, watch Netflix. You won't get far in an estate agent's if you're invisible."

Mr Bubb considered this and realised that the intellectual challenges of this conversation were too much for him this morning. He wondered how the estate agent had coped with her purple eyes.

"Good point Mo. Anyway, this came for you," he said, pulling a yellow post-it note from the wall and handing it over.

"Ah, thank you. I know I've said it before, but I'll say it again; this is much more civilised than the old way, with all those irritating incantations and pentagrams and what-not. It's all a touch too theatrical to my way of thinking. Derek still does it, mind."

"Derek?"

"You know him. Looks like an eighty year old man. I had tea with him just the other day, and the chap that served us called him that. Suits him, I think."

"Oily Derek, eh? He was in here the other day dressed in overalls or something. Wanted to know if I sold hats."

"He can be very odd sometimes, but I know what he's up to. He's got a new interest; something to do with trains. A bit nerdy, I think, but he used to go round quoting the Bible all the time, so it's an improvement I suppose."

"He did. What was all that about, the Bible stuff?"

"He said it was to "Know Your Enemy". He said, but I think he just found it funny. Anyway, let's look at this note."

An incredible amount of information was written on the yellow paper. Every time the demon calling herself Maureen turned it over there was something new to read. Eventually she stopped.

"It's a case of animal cruelty. That always gets the British going, have you noticed? They could chase each other up and down the street with pointy sticks and Joe Public would pass by whistling, as if nothing had happened. Don't want to get involved. Kick your dog? Woah! You'll need a pointy stick to keep the crowds at bay."

"Is that what this is? A kicked dog? Hardly seems worth you bothering to get away from the telly for."

"No, that was just an example. It's a horse that's been left to die in a field. Human law's taking way too long to deal with it and somebody has called down evil on the owner of the beast. As always, I thank you for being the go between and taking the messages from our….."

"…friends in low places. I know." Bert's heard it all before.

"Anyway, I must give you something for your trouble."

Mr Bubb rolls his eyes as she rummages in her bag. His expectations are low.

"Here! Do you like Cream Crackers?"

***

The old horse was growing weaker; too weak to stand now. Its field companions had left. The horse didn't know why they weren't there anymore, but horses are herd animals. Its solitude only added to the stress. Perhaps the man had come and taken them through the gate.

Pain, so much pain. It had been bad when he was standing, but now the pressure of his own body weight made it worse. Struggling to his feet was no longer achievable. Pain, and the discomfort of being in his own excrement, and his tail no longer being any discouragement to the swarms of flies.

It grew dark and then light again, more than once. At last, somebody was there. Not the man. Somebody with a different voice. He could sense their agitation, hear high pitched shrieks and then quieter words near his head, and then silence again.

The woman went in search of the owner, looking for help for this poor, distressed animal. She was met with an aggressive suggestion to mind her own business, that the horse was perfectly fine, that she should leave the property immediately.

A friend went with her, back to the horse, to attempt to encourage it to drink, or eat something, anything, while her husband eventually managed to persuade the police that there was an animal welfare issue for them to address. Late in the evening, they arrived at the field with a vet. The horse was dimly aware that it was becoming dark again. The man wasn't there.

The owner was hardly any more cooperative with the police than he was with the woman. He had lots of animals to take care of and it was hard to keep track of every little ailment. Before driving away, the vet informed the police officers that he would be happy to contribute historical information to any investigation, but he knew it would drag on for some time.

A Career Opportunity

"A what? Did you say trolley dolly?"

"Did you not hear me?"

"I heard you alright. I just can't believe you said it. I'm a qualified accountant, not a tea lady."

"You were a qualified accountant, back in the life that you're not a part of anymore."

"Thanks to you."

The demon turns quickly, angrily, his purple eyes glowing.

"When are you going to start taking responsibility for your own actions? Tell me that!"

"Alright! Okay! But four years in a chair? I've lost my family? I get offered a job as a tea lady? Isn't that a bit much?"

"Well I can't offer you the Catering Manager's job. That's already taken. How about I make you the Head of Customer Services? Would that make you happier?"

"What on earth are you talking about?"

He's calmer now. The glow diminishes.

"I think we're both talking at cross purposes here. Your punishment, I can see, is uppermost in your mind, yes?"

"Exactly!"

"It is written, "Foolishness is tied up in the heart of a boy." Or girl, I suppose. "The rod of discipline is what will remove it far from him." Or her, I suppose. Something like that."

"I'm not a child."

"You are to me, and a very foolish one. But listen, I've always prided myself on being inventively cruel and sadistic; no, please. I require no confirmation from you. But I try to be fair. Reasonable, you might say."

"Ha! I probably wouldn't say that."

"Put it another way. I believe in the idea of a statute of limitations. I know when enough's enough. That's why I terminated the contract on your friend Chris."

"He's no more my friend than you are, thank you very much."

"I think you may have to reconsider that at some point in the future. Are you going to eat that hash brownie?"

"What? No, it's cold now; you're very welcome to it. I'm struggling to keep up with this conversation. Are you actually suggesting there might be an end to this hell?"

"It's not hell. You wouldn't….."

"Alright, purgatory!"

"Not there either…"

"Do you have to be so fucking pedantic?"

"Oh look! You've been doing so well and you go and let yourself down like that."

"Please! Just answer the effing question."

"Yes."

"What? Yes, there might be an end…..?"

"Yes, woman! Try to keep up will you? I'm thinking about it, but it's not quite as easy as you may think. If you go back to your old life you'll be arrested for arson. Out of the frying pan, into the ongoing criminal investigation, you could say."

"I hadn't thought of that. But surely you can fix all that, can't you? You're always boasting about doing the impossible. There must be something you can do. I need to see how Greg is."

"Just a moment Ms Eager-When-It's-All-About-Me. There may be something I can do, but it rather depends on you helping me first."

"As a trolley dolly?"

"Exactly. Or Head of Customer Services, if you prefer"

"And if I do that, will you help me?"

"The incentive is, of course, performance related."

"Good grief! And where do I have to be this sufficiently good Head of Customer Services?"

"I'm going to hijack the Chinnor to Princes Risborough Railway."

Of all the things that she could have expected him to say in reply, that was nowhere near the top of her list.

"You clearly weren't expecting me to say that, I can tell. But listen. I was round at a friend's flat the other night, watching a bit of television. There was this thing on, about a group of people on a train that went round and round the world, ad infinitum. Preposterous concept, I know. But it got me thinking. I could do that."

Melanie's mind was reeling again; a vengeance demon goes to a friend's flat for a bit of telly? That was as mind-boggling as hijacking a railway.

"I've been on that. It doesn't go round the world."

"No, silly. It goes from Chinnor to Princes Risborough. Hence the name. It was the 'ad infinitum' possibility that I was thinking of."

"But it only takes about twenty five minutes to go from one end to the other."

"Well observed. And then it goes back. Up and down, up and down, up and down. Ad infinitum."

"Sounds appalling."

"Doesn't it just? So I'm going to mix business with

pleasure. I finally get to drive a steam train while you look after the passengers; serve them drinks and snacks, that sort of thing."

"That sounds even more appalling!"

"Ah, but the scenery's lovely, don't you think? And the passengers will be an interesting lot, trust me. One of them is the truck driver that knocked your husband off his bike."

Peace and Quiet

Darryl Clark backed his van up to the open gate. This was one of his favourite spots, nowhere near the town, his chance to get well away from all the hustle and bustle. Not a house in sight; just how he liked it. He turned the engine off and took a moment or two to enjoy the peace and solitude. He could hear a blackbird singing away another evening, distant sheep noises. Or were they goats? He didn't really know much about what goes on in the countryside.

He didn't consider himself particularly anti-social; the lads down at The Crown could confirm that, his cheerful smile rarely absent and his broad shoulders and powerful arms made him a shoe-in for the annual tug-of-war match. but he needed to be on his own right now. Unloading old tins of paint, cleaning chemicals and bags of broken plasterboard is not a spectator sport.

The farmer that owned the land was sick of people like Darryl, and equally sick of the injustice in the legal system that made him responsible for the cost of clearing this waste from his own land, even more complicated and expensive if it involved dangerous chemicals. It was absurd, he thought, that if he didn't clean them up he could be prosecuted for having these substances on his land. This evening things were going to be dealt with….differently.

Keen to try anything, he'd listened to an idea from his wife, whose book of the month club had come up with a very alternative suggestion. What the heck kind of book are they reading this month? he thought. His wife told him not to worry about that. She and the girls in The Coven, an old slight they had been happy to adopt, would see if there was anything they could do.

And so, in the gloom of the evening, Darryl didn't notice the pentagram traced in the dust. As he dropped the first couple of cans into the middle of it, the blackbird stopped singing. Darryl turned round to pick up a sack full of plasterboard fragments and was surprised to find himself standing on the footplate of a steam locomotive with a shovel in his hand. That wiped the smile from his face.

What's The Worst That Can Happen?

The demon realised that Charlie was calling to him;

"Phone call for you, Derek."

Melanie was left sitting on her bar stool, wondering if life could throw up any more twisted surprises and then wondering why she'd even bothered entertaining the question. Of course it could, and of course, it would. She could hear the demon (Derek? Couldn't get used to that) having what sounded like an argument with someone.

"I don't want them. It was my idea. I pick the passengers."

Some of the other customers in the café were starting to find this interesting, until he gave them the full benefit of his disturbing purple glare.

"Yes, of course it's a great idea, but don't bother flattering me.......Never mind about them being very deserving cases....Really? That's appalling! Even the Four Horsemen of the Apocalypse would have called a vet....Yes, there are still tickets left, but you have to do something for me. And one other thing; if you're sending me more passengers, then you can come with us.....No! You're not busy. You're a television addict."

He looked across at Melanie, who was looking very small and miserable for a tall person.

"Mo! You've got a spare room in that place of yours, haven't you? No, I only need the one. Does your landlord know about all your alterations? No, I wouldn't tell him, either….. After three then."

"Who was that?" Melanie asks without much enthusiasm. She was feeling extremely tired, in spite of four years in a chair. An overload of information and shocking revelations can do that. And she wasn't accustomed to having such a big breakfast either.

"A work colleague, I supposed you'd say."

"Human, or …like you?"

"Like me, sort of. Looks human, though; to you, anyway. Calls herself Maureen, or you can call her Mo, if she takes to you."

"A lady demon?"

"It's just a disguise. Anyway, she can put you up for the night."

"Whatever. I'm getting used to not having a choice anymore. But you have to tell me what this is all about. You can't just mention the truck driver and then walk away."

"I walked away because I had to answer the phone! Be fair. Look, let's walk and talk. Charlie's pretty tolerant, but we've only spent about fourteen pounds, so we can't occupy these stools all day. I'll take you to the park."

There was a brief, tense conversation with Charlie, who felt it was about time that Derek settled his tab, and then they stepped out into the sunshine.

Melanie had no idea where she was. The last place she could remember being in was a suburb of Birmingham, but this didn't look like that.

"Where are we exactly?"

"Where would you like to be?"

"I'd like to be home!"

"That's not convenient right now, as I've already told you. You're working for me. But while we talk, let's make this Oxford. I'll let you feel a bit closer to home. Won't that be nice?"

He took her across the road from the café and ushered her through the entrance to Christchurch Meadow. She couldn't decide if he was actually trying to be kind, or just showing off. Whichever, it was a bittersweet gesture; so near a home that she couldn't get to. She knew he wouldn't let her go.

"Is this really Oxford?"

"Yes, it's really Oxford. Thought you'd like it."

"So where have I been for the last four years?"

"Geographically, nowhere. The room with the chair is something I fabricated from somebody's dream."

"Whose dream? It's not one of mine."

"No, not one of yours. It was one of Chris Adwell's, if you must know. Now stop asking so many questions and walk."

Melanie is about to respond to that, but is distracted by something very strange about all the people around them.

"Just a minute! What's going on? Where have you taken me? Why are so many people wearing masks? It's like being in Tokyo."

And so, as they walked through the Meadow, he told her what she had missed over the last four years. He explained what the Pandemic had done to the world; the panic, the deaths, the vaccines, the lockdowns, the divisions. And he denied any responsibility for what happened, even though he admired the way in which so much despair had spread around the planet.

"It was like the Black Death back in the fourteenth century. That would have been so much more effective if they'd had air travel and foreign holidays. But this new one had nothing at all to do with us, although I understand that one of my colleagues was responsible for the circulation of dozens of conspiracy theories. It's amazing how sheep-like some people are when you plant an idea. Hilarious."

"You clearly think so. The Black Death? Just how long have you been around?"

"Oh long before that. Getting back at people has been part of being human since the beginning of time. Nothing's changed. The caveman comes home from the boar hunt to find another man dragging his woman round the floor of the cave by her hair, which is clearly not on, and he's upset. Can't have some other feller usurping his position in the home. That feller should be in his own home, dragging his own woman around, but unfortunately, he has a bigger cudgel. Or your next door neighbour's sabre-toothed tiger insists on defecating in your potato patch. So you look up the local mystic, and for the payment of a couple of pterodactyl eggs, you would be treated to a lot of impressive chanting and muttering and then that would call up one of us to do your dirty work for you. You know how it works, obviously. You've seen it."

"Don't remind me. Did any of my family get this, what is it….corona? I'm assuming you know."

"Your son Alex had it for a week or so; lots of coughing and feeling weak, like extreme man-flu, and he had to stay shut in his room, no contact with anybody else, because your husband was particularly vulnerable after he came out of hospital."

"That's how I remember Alex anyway. He hardly ever left his room except to visit the bathroom. I used to leave his meals outside the door and knock."

"And who would have known you were training him for how to cope in a pandemic? Well done! Great parenting skills."

"But Greg, didn't get it? He's okay"

"Yes, if you can call being pushed around in a wheelchair and having somebody visit every day to help him in and out of the bath, okay."

Melanie turns to him angrily.

"Do you have to be so cruel?"

"No, I don't have to be, but I've been doing it for such

a long time….."

There's a very awkward silence as they both realise this conversation has gone too far. They slowly walk on, past the Botanical Garden and emerge onto the High Street near Magdalen Bridge. Melanie looks to the right, across the bridge, towards The Plain. With a shudder, she turns to the left and they continue towards the city. She wonders if she will see anybody she knows. Or what might happen if they recognise her. Oxford's the sort of city where you can bump into people you know all the time, but today nobody seems to see her at all. She checks her reflection in a shop window, just to make sure she has one; the demon's taken everything else. In her current mood, the gleaming spires might as well have been factory chimneys for all the attraction they had.

She is finally the one to break the silence.

"So what's this job you want me to do? If I can't avoid it, that is."

"You can't. So, as I told you, I intend to mix business with pleasure. I've told you about the pleasure side of it. I'm going to drive a steam engine. Aren't they just amazing? All that power and steam and noise. And heat and flames and…."

He tails off, a faraway look in his eyes.

"Sorry, I was….anyway; don't you agree?"

"I think that was more Greg's thing than mine. I was more into horses. A galloping horse.. That's power and grace, if you ask me."

"Without the flames though. Horses, eh? There are going to be some very interesting conversations on the train, I think."

"Who's going to be on the train? The truck driver, yes?"

He nods. "Well that's the business part of it, you see. I have a collection of people who, it has been deemed, have proved themselves worthy of punishment; my kind of punishment. So I'm going to take them out for the day, and the next day, and the next day…."

"Ad infinitum?"

"That's the plan. Good, isn't it?" She doesn't look so sure.

"Am I there, ad infinitum, too?"

He smiles. "I told you; I'm working on that. And it does depend on your cooperation. I haven't told you the worst part yet."

"Worse than meeting that truck driver?"

"Yes, and even worse than looking at that same bit of the Chilterns for weeks, months, possibly years on end. No, I've decided that the passengers will have their families with them. I hope you like children."

No Place Like Home

Melanie would normally have enjoyed a stroll through the city of Oxford, browsing in the Covered Market, lunch on the roof of the Westgate Centre, that sort of thing. But not today. It was like another world now. Today she just felt miserable, and overwhelmed with information that provided her with as many questions as answers. But at least she wasn't sitting in that damn chair, which was one of the few positives; maybe the only one. Her situation now was like being in prison, in spite of walking about in the city streets. She knew the demon wouldn't let her leave and she knew, reluctantly admitted, that this was her own fault for contacting him in the first place. But she missed Greg and the kids; they must be less than five miles away if they were at home, and it was even worse knowing that Greg needed looking after; by her, not by a string of carers calling in every day, however good and professional they might be. It wasn't fair!

They eventually finished up outside a large, bay-windowed house in one of the roads leading off Walton Street, in Jericho. Probably at some time in its history a sizeable family home, but now divided up into flats, it stood out from some of the neighbouring properties by appearing to be freshly painted and having a very neat and tidy little front garden. The demon pressed the button for the doorbell and very soon a hand pulled back the orange and yellow curtains at a first floor window.

"Maureen's flat," said the demon, answering the question that Melanie hadn't cared enough to ask.

A buzz and a click, and they were in. The demon calling herself Maureen met them on the first floor landing.

"Duytuvitf"

"Iuhiuh Sgb! Good to see you again. But not in front of the humans, if you don't mind. Let's just stick to Maureen."

"Of course; *Derek*. And you must be Melanie. My word, you *are* a pretty young thing, although you do look a bit tired. Come in and sit down."

Melanie was well past the horns-and-a-tail concept of what a demon should look like, so the rather dowdy woman in late middle-age that greeted her with a smile and a hand to shake came as no surprise. She had thought at one point that she'd never want to sit down again, but she realised she was mentally exhausted, even too tired to react to Maureen's patronising words. She suddenly realised that she'd just missed her fiftieth birthday, and Greg's. Their planned celebratory skiing trip to Boulder could never happen now. She allowed herself to be ushered towards a large armchair, which she was horrified to see was identical to the one she'd recently vacated.

"I'm not sitting in that! I'll sit on the floor, if that's alright with you."

For once, 'her' demon looked sympathetic.

42

"A little tactless, Maureen. Not everybody appreciates our sense of humour, I've learned. But, my word, this is a cosy little place you've got here."

"It is now! It was a complete dump when I got the keys. The paint outside was all cracked and flaking off and the front garden full of rubbish. I did all that this morning when I knew you were coming. Cheated a bit, though, to be honest."

"Tools of the trade, obviously. It would be silly not to. But look; our guest is asleep, which is probably a good thing. Big day tomorrow."

"I envy these humans sometimes. Must be nice not to be awake twenty-four seven, a thousand per millennium."

"But we're too busy. I had almost a three decade waiting list at one point. We're becoming far too "go-to" in my opinion. I was reading that one in six of the population of this country claims to be pagan, and one in ten of those reckon they're witches."

"I would love to see that on a Venn diagram; see if it overlaps with the ones that claim to be Jedi! So look; I'm sorry I foisted a couple of my victims onto you, but I know you'll cope. You've got plenty of space, after all. But come on; while she's asleep, I'll show you around."

'Derek' led the way back into the living room some hours later, brushing feathers from his sleeves.

"Well I'm most impressed. Your games room is especially good. It must be years since I last used a crossbow. And that chicken dinner was superb."

"Thank you. I thought so too, but they clearly don't enjoy the chase as much as we do. Ah! Now where has our young friend got to?"

"You didn't lock the front door, did you?"

"Oops! Silly me. I don't know. You offer somebody your hospitality.....How rude!"

**

"I've got away!" thought Melanie, as she ran down the street back towards the city.

"Don't kid yourself." thought the demon, as he settled down with a glass of red wine to watch a bit of telly. The demon calling herself Maureen placed a third empty glass on the small table in the middle of the living room.

They were only half an hour into Saw III when the doorbell rang.

"Pause that, if you don't mind, Iuhiuh Sgb. I'll get the door."

"Bother! I really enjoy these DIY shows. Full of useful tips."

Melanie pushes the door open as soon as she hears the click and practically runs up the stairs. She hadn't gone very far along her escape route before the complete pointlessness of what she was attempting dawned on her. She had no money, no phone, couldn't go to the police or home for the reasons the demon had already reminded her of, notwithstanding the fact that he could probably take her back to square one with a click of his fingers. Compliance was her only course, but she would let him know, in no uncertain terms, that she didn't have to like it, and that was the mood she was in when she thrust open the living room door at the top of the stairs.

Whatever she was going to say was put on hold as she was greeted by the demon smiling at her, in his outstretched hand a large glass of red wine.

"Ah Melanie. You look as if you could do with this. It's an excellent Cabernet Sauvignon. I know it's one of your favourites. And Mo has done some nibbles for you."

Maureen comes through from the kitchen with a plate of cheese and biscuits and a few olives in a matching bowl.

"Here you are dear. I'm afraid it's all I've got. I don't often have guests you see. Now come and sit down and watch a bit of telly with us."

"And perhaps something with a little less gore in it for our guest? Countdown, perhaps? That doesn't usually have much bloodshed."

Melanie took the glass almost as a reflex action, never having knowingly refused a glass of red wine, even in times of stress. But she couldn't have given a damn about which consonants or vowels were being selected and displayed on the television screen. The demon spoke just as she was about to say what she thought.

"You're upset, we can tell."

"Upset?! Upset doesn't even begin to cover it. I'm bloody steaming! I can't go anywhere without you pulling me back, I'm being forcibly kept away from my family, and they need me and…..I just feel humiliated. And I'm mad at myself for getting into this mess in the first place."

"Well that's progress. A bit of contrition at last. There's hope for you yet."

"Oh *is* there?" Melanie's reaction is sarcastic. "You've given me hints, but that's it. If I help you, you said, you might let me go."

"I did say that, and I said any favourable outcome for you is performance related; remember that too. So I need to see a bit more interest and enthusiasm, instead of listening to you whining on about how disappointed you are with your lot. Do you understand?"

A staring match ensues, Melanie tight-lipped and blowing hard down her nostrils. Her belligerence finally subsides, pale blue eyes being no match for a pair of blazing purple ones.

"Yes, I understand."

"Good! Now Maureen has picked out a rather fetching uniform for you to wear, and, if all goes to plan, I'm considering a convenient date for you to return to your life."

"You have? Don't I get a say in that? Because I was wondering if I could make a suggestion…"

Dinner And A Show

"For a start the colour's all wrong; bright red doesn't work with my hair. If I'm going to do this thing, I might as well at least look right. This just makes me look like a Christmas decoration."

Instantly the outfit becomes turquoise.

"That's what you were thinking, isn't it, dear?"

"Don't tell me *you're* reading my mind too! So you'll know I think the skirt's too short. I'm fifty, not twenty. And I don't like this silk scarf thing. Can't stand having things around my neck."

Once again, Melanie's criticisms are instantly addressed, except…

"Oh no! Not the hat as well. That thing makes me look like a Thunderbirds puppet!"

"What do you think, Derek?" Maureen asks the demon his opinion as he walks into the dressing room.

"Great job, Mo. And I think the hat stays, definitely. It gives her an air of authority. She's going to need that."

"I think she looks very impressive; five feet eleven inches tall, blue eyed blonde and in that uniform; very imposing."

"As impressive as humans ever get, I suppose. Now, come back to the living room. There's somebody you need to meet."

"Not another bloody demon!"

"Ha ha! No, and let me tell you, you never want to meet the Bloody Demons. Their methods are quite different to mine, I assure you. No, he's human, like you; well mostly," he said, with a theatrical wink to his fellow demon. "He's our Catering Manager, and he has, I think you might say, unique qualifications. Certainly in this day and age anyway. Come on!"

Melanie followed, wondering why there was always, *always* something cryptic about everything he said to her; always something new to figure out. Or perhaps he just got some kind of pleasure out of her obvious confusion, a sort of mental one-upmanship; keep the human in the dark. It also occurred to her that she hadn't interacted with another human, excepting the ones she'd passed in the streets of Oxford earlier in the day, but not properly, for a long time. She had mixed feelings about meeting one now. A uniquely qualified catering manager who was mostly human? What the hell did that mean?

Sitting quite comfortably in the armchair that Melanie had refused earlier was a rather chubby little man, in his forties, she estimated, a swarthy, dark complexion on his round face. Possibly he was from one of the countries on the north side of the Mediterranean; hard for her to pinpoint. Maybe Italy, she speculated. He had crinkly black hair and a nose that seemed too big, out of balance with his other features. A Roman nose? The swarthy face broke into a smile as soon as the door opened. His grey two piece suit seemed to be struggling in some areas, straining to contain the man within. He wore a black patch with little sparkly diamanté jewels over his left eye, which didn't go with the suit at all. Either the suit was borrowed or the eye patch was, Melanie speculated. His general look was of someone whose business activities, at some point in his life, may have fallen well short of the strict criteria allowed by his local Godfather. As soon as he saw his fellow guest and apparently soon-to-be colleague, he jumped to his feet, although 'jump' was probably what he'd intended to do. In reality, it was more of a struggle than he clearly would have liked, she judged from his expression. He managed to haul himself upright and eventually stabilised himself.

"Jeez, man. Ah still can't get used t'this peg. Ne'mind. Wot've you got 'ere and where d'ye find it?...... Very tasty! Totally pret!"

The accent could have been a blend of West Country, Cockney, faux Caribbean; very hard to narrow down on the strength of that startling introduction. But what was clear to Melanie was that it was offensive. Chauvinistic and downright rude! *It?* How *dare* he!

"What do you mean, pret?"

"Short for pret a manger. It means…."

"I know what it means. We don't have to put up with sexist remarks like that in this day and age."

"You will when I'm from."

"I'm sorry. That doesn't make any sense. What are you on about?"

The man turns to address the demon.

"She's not on page, is she? You didn't info her yet?"

Melanie turned to face the demon too, seething at the lack of respect for a twenty-first century woman.

"I'm not working with him! He's talking about me as if I'm a piece of meat!"

"Oh, don't say that! Permit me to do the introductions, and then I'll explain. Mr Jimbo DiRisso, meet Mrs Melanie Rainham. And vice versa, obviously."

Mr DiRisso extends a hand which Melanie refuses even to look at, as she stands there with her arms tightly folded.

"Needs a birra tenderising this 'un, wouldn't you say?"

Melanie whirls round to face him, practically spitting with fury:

"How dare you?! You disgusting little man!"

"Woah! Fulla spirit though. Like it!"

The demon holds up his hands, and in a booming voice that fills the airspace and swamps the developing argument, commands,

"Mister DiRisso! Kindly zip it for a moment, while I explain your presence here." And Melanie is somewhat gratified to see that the zip idea is applied literally, as it had been with her earlier in the day.

"That's better. Now! Mrs Rainham. I will provide some background details for you. You commented earlier that

I'm always busy. The devil makes work for idle hands, although I suppose that's a bit of a mixed metaphor in my case. Ha! Hadn't really thought of that before. Anyway… I was very busy until your daughter summoned me; busy in the year 2050."

"Good grief! That's not where you're planning to put me, is it? Not 2050?"

"Oh no. I can go backwards too. Don't interrupt woman! Anyway; the world will be rather a different place by 2050 and I was, or is it will be? hhmm…. let's go with was. I was asked to produce a game show for holovision. It's like television, but without the television. It's my own idea….. Stars In Their Pies, it's called."

"But we've already had Stars In Their Eyes. That wasn't your idea."

"I didn't say Eyes. I said Pies. It's a celebrity cannibal cooking program. Last one dining is the winner."

"What?! That's disgusting."

"You may say that, but, as I said, the world in 2050 is very different, but, to be fair, you've already had shows where a group of socially diverse, you might say challenged, people are locked in a house until somebody emerges as the winner, inflicting all kinds of damage on the others along the way. Or a show about people whose only discernible talent is their ability to twist the English language into something they've developed along their local estuary."

"But they don't kill each other!"

"More's the pity. Let me tell you something about your future. All the big talk of being carbon neutral, or better, by 2050 will come to nothing. Everybody will spend so much time and energy trying to avoid World War Three that they will be rather distracted from lofty environmental ideals. If you're planning to move into a retirement home with a view of the sea about then, I would suggest going no further south than Reading."

"I don't believe you!"

"In that case, you'll just have to wait and see, I suggest. But the point of what I'm telling you is that the world is going to get a lot more, how shall I put it?.....brutal; extremely basic in its quest for escape from the horrors of reality."

"Yes, but cannibalism? That's not an escape from horror. That *is* horror."

"No. That's entertainment. And the public have a taste for it, even when their names went into a hat for the Pro-Am events."

"What?! And you thought this up? Sick!"

"Just catering to public demand. And talking of catering…."

"Hang on! My kids will only be in their forties by then. They'll be younger than me. I can't imagine them wanting that kind of twisted crap, ever."

"Oh they don't have to like it. But if their name comes out of the hat…."

"No! There must be some way of stopping it. That doesn't have to be the future, surely."

"Well I'll leave you to work that out, shall I? Meanwhile, we have a train to catch. I think a pleasant chug through the countryside might be what everybody needs right now."

"Mmmhh!"

"Oh sorry, Mister DiRisso. I almost forgot you. Permission to speak granted."

"Ta, sport. Can I just say, thanks fer saving me life back there."

"What does he mean?"

"He means, Melanie, that a baying mob was after his blood. He was the winning finalist in the competition and he beat the favourite, a very promising film starlet. Her relatives are poor losers. Besides, we need somebody to do the cooking on the train, don't we."

"Not for me! Jesus! I'm vegan from this minute onwards."

"Y'ask me, they was just bothered about 'er earning potential. Very poor losers."

"Possibly true. She's not as tall as she used to be, so that's her dancing career gone. And thanks to that interesting little starter you came up with, singing and speaking parts are no longer an option."

"Ha ha! An' it cost me an arm an' a leg to win, don't forget."

Melanie clasps her hand to her face. "I think I'm going to be sick."

"Yes, dear. I think you are," says Maureen. "There's a bathroom through here, and a bedroom with a lock on the door."

"Good thinking, Mo. Now get some sleep, if you can, Melanie. We have a very pleasant railway journey planned for the morning."

"Yeah. D'ya think we'll all be chuffed to bits."

"Zip it, Jimbo!"

"Mmmhhh!"

Tickets to Ride

Chelsea Clark was having a really stressful day with the kids, and she'd only been in from work for an hour. She'd picked up her youngest from the childminder, who also looked a bit stressed. Chelsea never knew why anybody would pick that as a job, although she was grateful that somebody had! It was bad enough looking after her own kids; she couldn't imagine that looking after anybody else's children would be much fun. Her little Mia was challenging; cute, but a real live wire.

Mia was wearing off her energy now by winding up her big brother, Charlie. He'd been cute too, once. But now he was twelve, almost thirteen, and a big lad, like his father. Unlike his father, who was the life and soul of the parties they very rarely managed to get to these days, he'd become morose and moody, self-isolating in his bedroom long before it was thought of as a medical precaution. Online gaming with his mates had taken priority over doing stuff with the family. She hoped that's what he was doing with the internet anyway. He wasn't a bad kid really. He still had the capacity to surprise her with a home-made Mother's Day card.

But this evening they were just bickering and making too much noise, arguing at the top of the stairs and at the top of their voices. She needed a drink, and tomorrow, she decided as she unscrewed the gin bottle, she needed to get them out of the house. Darryl hadn't come in from work yet. She was used to starting the drink without him; self employed people don't really do nine-to-fives, he always told her. But now and again, she wondered if he maybe was seeing somebody else. There's irregular hours and then there's creeping home in the wee small hours of the morning. She didn't feel very glamorous any more, what with a long shift at the petrol station plus all the housework and dealing with their demanding kids. But then Darryl had lost his appeal too, with his beer belly and his grimy work clothes that he never thought to change when he got in. If she couldn't be moved to find him all that charming, she couldn't imagine any other woman coming to a different conclusion.

In the bathroom, she runs her fingers through her dull brown hair, which used to be her crowning glory, as the expression goes. But right now it looks a bit lifeless after a hard day at work, and smells somewhat of coffee from the machine that sits too close to where she usually works in the petrol station's shop. The face that looks back at her from the mirror is still attractive, she thinks. *("Am I still pretty, Darryl? You never tell me.")* Two kids and two jobs have taken their toll on her mindset. Her pride in her children and her major contribution to the family's finances helps keep her self-esteem intact, but her confidence in her looks has taken a battering.

She and Darryl used to be such an impressive couple, she with her hourglass curves, and makeup subtly applied, a benefit of professional training, and he with his wide shoulders, imaginatively tattooed forearms and winning smile. She hastily carried out some repair work on her mascara and stared hard at the mirror as she tried to remember the last time she'd seen his winning smile, and then wondered if somebody else might be seeing it instead.

But where the heck was he? Sod him! She'd make her own plans for tomorrow and he would just have to fit in. She would take the kids out herself; somewhere they hadn't been for ages. Chelsea went to the bottom of the stairs and bellowed to make herself heard.

"Charlie! Mia! For goodness' sake! Listen! We're going out tomorrow. You two need a day out of here, I think."

"Going where? Do I have to?"

"Yes, Charlie. You have to."

And then, out of nowhere, the thought comes into her head, "We're going to the Chinnor Railway."

"What's that, Mum?"

"It's like a real life Thomas the Tank Engine, Mia. You were too young to remember the last time we went."

"Will it be like the books?"

"I think so."

"Cool!" When did four year-olds start saying cool? Copying her dad, Chelsea thought.

"Lame." Charlie's reaction is what she'd come to expect lately. "I'm staying here."

"You are most certainly not staying here. There'll be nobody here to keep an eye on you. Your Dad's meeting us there."

Why did she just say that? They hadn't even discussed going there. She had only just thought of the idea herself.

57

"Well can I take my laptop then?"

"Oh if it keeps you from moping around all day, yes?"

But Chelsea was only half engaged with answering Charlie. She couldn't think why she'd suggested going on the train when her first thought was the pictures and a pizza.

***

Tony Barnes had a lot on his mind too. The pressures of running his farm; the paperwork, the staff shortages, the debts, and now this impending court case. That bloody interfering woman. Of course he hadn't meant for the horse to die. He just had so much to do all the time and now, to cap it all, his silly wife, Annabel, was standing behind him as he sat at the breakfast table, her hands over his eyes, singing "Happy Birthday" and telling him she had a surprise for him.

He'd forgotten it was his birthday. Fifty-bloody-four, was it? Sometimes he felt like he was twenty years past that.

"I haven't got time to go back to bed, if it's that kind of surprise."

Her hands were quickly removed from his face. The petite and prim Annabel had never liked innuendo, however subtle.

"No, not that kind of surprise," she says, icily. Pity, he thought. Something else he was always too distracted for. "No, we're going on a train."

"What? I haven't got time to go on any bloody train either."

"Oh come on! It's your birthday, Tony. We've got enough staff to run the petting zoo for the day, and you need to get away from all this worry. So that's what we're doing!"

He knew it was pointless arguing: "Sorry, Pet. I don't want to sound ungrateful, but not bloody London again. I bloody hate the place."

"Well you do sound ungrateful. But no, it's not bloody London again, although I'd quite like to go there. It's bloody Chinnor."

"Chinnor? What the railway?"

"Yes, the railway. You're going to meet up with some old mates."

Working on the steam railway was just another one of the things that he didn't have time to think about these days, but he remembered now. Twenty years ago he'd been a very enthusiastic volunteer in the group that had worked so hard to restore what was basically a giant train set. He'd done painting, carpentry, reupholstering, even tried on the Station Master's hat a couple of times.

"What do you mean, old mates?"

"Some of the people you used to work with will be there. You remember Bill? The Station Master? Chief Nerd, you used to call him."

Even while she's telling him this Annabel is puzzled. She had gone online yesterday to book tickets for a train to

Birmingham (*no, not bloody London. I got that right.*) and a concert at the Symphony Hall and instead she'd reserved a compartment on the Chinnor to Princes Risborough Railway.

***

Gary Fotherby's mobile rang; the theme from Knight Rider.

"Gaz! Get yer fat and lazy arse out of bed. I've got a van load for yer."

Gary swore that one day he'd swing for that bloke, but for now he'll have to keep schtum. He needed the cash in hand and there was no way he could get a proper driving job, not with his licence having been taken off him. In Gary's favour, had an independent observer dared to venture into his bedroom, they would have seen that Garys arse was anything but fat. He was a scrawny little man, in his late twenties, with very close-cropped hair and large holes in his ear lobes which hed been expanding for cosmetic reasons. He thought the look was great and was happy to bad-mouth anyone who dared to say otherwise.

So as a result of the phone-call, he finds himself driving a white Transit full of boxes of who-knew-what stuff and heading for the Chinnor to Princes Risborough Railway station. And what's that ahead? Not another sodding clown dithering about on a bike! What's he doing? That's no way to take a mini roundabout!

Gary opens his window as he narrowly avoids the back wheel of the bike. He really can't afford to hit another one.

"You should get some lessons, mate!"

"Piss off, wanker!"

As the van pulls away up the hill towards the station Gerald shouts after it:

"It's alright for you! You wanna try riding this thing with half a bleeding ton of spuds on the front."

He still can't make the gears work and decides to get off and push the last couple of hundred yards up the hill to the station.

Happy Days

Whoever decided, in 1965, that the Chiltern Hills, along the Oxfordshire, Buckinghamshire border, should be designated an Area Of Outstanding Natural Beauty was not wrong. The extensive deciduous woodlands and a network of footpaths and bridleways make it a great place for walkers, cyclists and horse riders to enjoy the great outdoors. Since 1989, the breeding program for the hitherto almost extinct Red Kite has created another attraction in the area as birdwatchers come to see these magnificent birds of prey, or these complete bloody nuisances if you're trying to dine *al fresco*. Hang on to your baguette!

Not all of the Outstanding things in the Chilterns were either Natural or Beautiful, the Chinnor Cement Works being a case in point. It provided employment in the area for almost a century from 1908. The demolition of its chimney drew a large crowd, as controlled explosions will, the onlookers possibly feeling a mixture of empowerment and regret as the familiar edifice fell sideways. The big attraction in the area now is the peaceful wildlife reserve that has developed around the lakes that have filled the old quarries in the shadow of the steep side of the hills. Flocks of birds have learned to include these on their feeding and nesting routes, and smaller flocks of twitchers have learned that it's a good place to bring their binoculars.

The other big attraction in the area is the Chinnor to Princes Risborough Railway, which operates its steam and classic diesel engines from a site adjacent to the old cement works, and its short journey along the base of the hills to Princes Risborough and back is a huge draw for train enthusiasts and families looking for a day out. The old train station has been rebuilt by the volunteers that run the railway and provides a suitable taste of nostalgia.

It was a Sunday morning, just before eleven, and the management at the railway station should have been gratified to see the number of people waiting to catch their train; strong ticket sales in this good late Spring weather. The platform was seething. Some of the people on it were seething too, most notably Ginny Tucker, a very harassed mother of three small children. She had just spotted her ex-boyfriend in the distance, the useless shit that hadn't paid her anything for their kids for most of the last year. He seemed to be unloading boxes from the back of a van. What an amazing coincidence that they'd both turned up here at the same time and, she thought, an excellent opportunity for her to give him a piece of her mind, backed up with the threat that, if he didn't pull his bloody finger out and show some sense of responsibility, she would shop him for all his illegal driving jobs. But she realised her immediate problem, though, was that she had three under-sixes to look after, and she was being helped into a carriage by an overly helpful platform attendant. One of the kids had already been lifted through the door. She didn't know whether to thank the guard or tell him to mind his own flippin' business. He didn't look as if he'd be particularly receptive to either comments. Whatever, her chance to speak to Gaz was gone.

Somebody else that was none too happy was Tony

Barnes. His wife had failed to mention that part of the deal for having the petting zoo looked after by their son and daughter-in-law was that they had to take the grandchildren out for the day. That wasn't Tony's idea of his birthday treat, but he resolved to bear it stoically, or at least make all the expected noises of a male grandparent. Looking on the bright side, these two had progressed beyond the age of climbing onto his lap and covering his clothes in sticky fingerprints.

Meeting his old mate Bill had been a bit of a strange experience too. The feller had seemed really distant, rather disengaged; no reaction to being called 'Chief Nerd'. In fact all the volunteers at the station were like that. It was only a hobby, for goodness sake; thought they'd at least look like they were enjoying themselves.

"I'm sorry Tony," Bill explained, "But we can't figure out what's happened to our usual driver. This old bloke's taken his place but we can't seem to get near him to find out what's going on."

The substitute engine driver was indeed an old man, eighty if he was a day, who looked very pleased with himself, fussing over the locomotive as if it was his favourite toy. He was accompanied by a bewildered looking, much younger man with a shovel. The driver was talking to a rather dowdy looking lady of an indeterminate vintage, probably about Tony's age, and a tall, elegant blonde woman in a turquoise suit that made her look like an air hostess, or whatever it was politically correct to call them these days; Tony couldn't remember. Bugger political correctness! The woman was exhibiting some very negative body language towards the fourth member of this group, a chubby little fellow who moved with apparent discomfort, as if he'd injured his leg, or possibly his back; Tony knew all about the pain of sciatica. The feller looked like he might've been Italian. Every time he moved, the woman made sure there were at least two metres between them, with a look full of daggers to keep it that way. Still social distancing perhaps. Not so many people on the train are bothering with masks now, he noticed.

The older woman took the engine driver to one side and a heated conversation commenced. She pointed to a group of elderly looking men at the far end of the platform. They were dressed in dark suits, clearly wearing wigs, and one of them was clutching a guitar like a drowning man hangs onto a life-raft.

"What do they call themselves?"

"The Cheatles.. They're a tribute band for…"

"Don't tell me! I've worked it out already. The answer is no! I decide how the passengers are punished. I didn't intend that I should suffer too."

"They were so far away from the high note in 'I Saw Her Standing There' that somebody called down evil upon them…"

"I'm not surprised."

"….and you know the drill. I'm stuck with them."

"No! I agreed to the horse killer, but this is too much. They'll just have to…..hang on! Is that a Gibson Les Paul one of them's holding?"

"A what?"

"That guitar. It's beautiful. I've got an idea that perhaps we can help them after all. Follow me."

The quartet looks towards the approaching engine driver, thinking that here's somebody who can explain their baffling situation. Being cajoled onto a railway station platform by a woman who is old enough to be one of their groupies made no sense at all. One minute they were going through their repertoire in a rapidly emptying pub, the next they were....where exactly? The sign says Chinnor. Where the heck is that? Perhaps this old chap walking over from the train, with the driver's gloves, and with the strange purple eyes.....

"Good morning, gentlemen. You're all looking a bit confused, and I must admit to being confused myself. My friend Maureen here, tells me that you've been booked on to entertain my passengers."

That's news to Maureen, and obviously to the band.

"Frank?" says the man holding the precious guitar. "Did you book this?"

"Must've done, Lloyd. Don't remember it though, to be honest."

"That's your age, mate. That's why we write the set list in such big letters!"

"Gentlemen! Never mind all that and your internal politics. The point is we don't need you. So I'm sorry for your inconvenience, but I'd be more than happy to drop you somewhere. The train goes to the mainline station at Princes Risborough, if that helps. A train or a taxi to wherever you need to go. On the house."

"Well that's very decent of you, squire."

"And we'll take good care of your guitar for you."

"Never leaves me sight, pal. Cost me five grand that did."

"I can well imagine. I've had some fine instruments myself, down the years."

"You're a guitarist too?"

"Not yet. But I used to play a Stradivarius a few years ago."

"Wow! That must've been a valuable antique. I'd be scared to handle something like that."

"No, it was brand new when I had it. Now come along. We need to get you on board before all the seats are taken."

***

With two lots of roadworks on her drive to the station, Chelsea Clark was worried she would miss the train, but she was there with at least five minutes to spare and had time to take a breather. Mia was bursting with enthusiasm when she saw the steam engine.

"Mummy! It's Thomas!"

Charlie, dragging his feet, is less excited. Getting excited is not cool. And then he sees an old metal sign advertising Corona.

"Hey Mum! Is this where the virus started? It looks dodgy enough. Hey wait, will you! It says 'Sparkling Drinks and Fruit Squashes'."

"Well there you go. I'm always telling you those fizzy drinks are bad for you. Now come on, and mind you don't drop that laptop. I can't afford another one. We need to find your Dad."

Mia has already spotted him:

"Daddy! Daddy!"

Darryl looks at the demon, points to his daughter, and the demon gives a nod of assent. Darryl puts his shovel down. He's as surprised to see his family here as he was to find himself on the footplate of a locomotive, but he's glad to see his little girl.

"Angel!" He bends down to scoop her up, looking over her shoulder to see the other two approaching. "Chelsea! Love. What are you doing here?"

"And it's good to see you too. See, Charlie; I said he'd be here."

"Cool…"

"But I don't understand. How did you know that? I didn't even know I was coming."

"I just knew. I don't know how. I don't get why they've got you working in the engine though."

Darryl and Chelsea stand and look at each other, trying to come up with an explanation that makes sense. Nothing.

"This is….."
"……weird."

"Hey Dad! That man over there. Is he like a pirate or something?"

"Charlie! That's rude. You shouldn't talk about disabled people like that."

"Yeah, right Mum. But is he, Dad? Cool eye patch."

***

An argument in public is a fascinating thing, a combination of 'let's hear every word' and 'don't get involved, dear'. Passengers on the periphery of the crowd were distracted by a noisy altercation that was taking place at the back of the white van, attracting listeners at first when the words carried on the breeze were "don't want any trouble mate" but parents decided to move their families more rapidly towards the waiting carriages when they heard "show some fucking consideration". Nobody actually saw how the engine driver managed to move through the crowd on the platform, but suddenly he was between the warring factions, holding them apart with a strength that was impressive for such an old man. The result was that Gary and Gerald found themselves working together, albeit in sullen discomfort, loading the contents of their respective vehicles into a storage area at the back of the train. They were still there when the train departed, both wrestling with the locked door and blaming each other for having buggered up the mechanism.

***

Fresh from negotiating the uneasy truce between the two delivery men, the demon turned his attention to Melanie and Jimbo.

"Correct me if I'm wrong, but you two don't seem to

be getting along very well. I can't have that. We need some professionalism. So what I suggest is, while I'm taking this train up and down the line for the first run, you both go and have a coffee together and sort out your differences."

"Forget that! I'm not having coffee with a misogynistic cannibal."

"Oh yes you are. That's if Mr DiRisso here is prepared to sit down with a cat-poisoning arsonist."

"She's a what?" That's got Jimbo's attention. Melanie had forgotten about the cat.

"You'd forgotten about the cat, I see. Wouldn't want that to get out amongst the passengers, would we? Now go and do as you're told. Through here, now." And he leads them into the station coffee shop.

"Charlie! Get these two whatever they're drinking and put it on my tab."

"About your tab, Derek….." But the demon has gone, leaving Melanie open-mouthed. Surely Charlie was…….

Jimbo DiRisso is already heading for a seat, grinning all over his face; his infuriating face.

"Don't look so smug, you pervert."

"Ha! Yer charm bunny. Like to make things hot, do yer?"

"He would have to tell you that! It wasn't a regular thing….look! I don't have to explain myself to you. It's not like I eat people for entertainment. That's disgusting."

"You're right. It is. But public demand, you know."

This last statement comes without any trace of the bizarre mixture of accents that Melanie found so grating. He suddenly sounds very 'Home Counties'.

"Hang on! What's happened to your accent?"

"Oh that? My stage persona. Out there, isn't it?"

"Finally! We agree on something. But I still don't understand how you can do what you do."

"It's 2050. You had to be there. Will have to have been there…..? I give up."

"I'm glad I'm not."

"Only twenty-eight years to go. Probs, you will be. Bout forty something, I'm guessing?"

Flattering, she thought, but she wasn't about to give him the pleasure of knowing that. She decided to change the subject.

"This cookery thing you were on…..I can't believe I said cookery…..you said it was a celebrity competition. What's your claim to fame?"

"Investigative journalism."

"You're kidding me! My first impression was that you couldn't read or write."

That earns a fleeting pained expression.

"Ouch and thanks heaps. But that look can take people

off-guard, you see. Safe talking to me, they reckon. Well, it worked until I became really famous anyway. Started hamming it up big for the shows. Demands larger than life, you copy?"

It wasn't too hard to figure out most of his verbal shorthand, and Melanie thought that dropping the accent made him less bombastic; not quite humble, but heading in that direction.

"What did you write that made you famous?"

From outside come the sounds of carriage doors slamming, a whistle and the steam locomotive straining to haul away its load of passengers to who-knew-what fate. Without being asked, Charlie places a cappuccino and a black Americano on the table; "Your usual. You're welcome."

"Ah! Good man, Charlie. So; writing. Couple of best-sellers really: 'The Assassination of Saint Greta' and 'Room on the Broom? Escaping a Quidditch Gambling Cartel'.

"Jesus! You don't mean Greta…..?"

"Fraid so. Not everybody feels the same about environmental issues, especially the ones who make money out of ignoring them."

"Nothing's going to change. That's what the demon said. Are we really headed for World War Three?"

"No, not by 2050 anyway, but damnty close. And the powers will spend so much time and money on trying not to off each other that there's no time for elses. I remember; everybody's talking about global warming and rising sea levels now, but what's that old saying? 'The road to hell is paved with good intentions'. Hey! I suppose we could always ask our friend, Derek? That makes me laugh…yeah, we could ask him about road surfaces on the way to hell. I'm sure he would have a sm'answer. What do you make of the old sm'arse? Funny old stick, eh?"

"Funny?! He's a monster. You think somebody that thinks up a cannibal cooking show is funny? Look what he's done to you. I can't wait to get away from him."

"About that; I haven't figured out what you're doing here in the first place. What's he got you here for? I can't wait to hear about the cat poisoning and the arson."

"I really don't want to talk about it, if you don't mind."

"I don't mind at all. The investigative journalist side of me just now has no outlet anyway. Stifled! Without that I'm just a nosey-parker. But getting away. Do you really think you can? Because I need out of here too."

"I hope so. He's practically promised that I will. I need to get back to my family."

"Promised, you say? Y'know, you say he's a monster, but I think he's a monster of his word. He said he would get me out of the frying pan, so to speak, and he did. And here I am. At least most of me's here."

"So why do you need to get away?"

"I need to find myself."

"Huh! You're the last person I would expect to find on a journey of spiritual enlightenment or self discovery or whatever you want to call it."

"No. I mean I need to find myself, literally. Somewhere out there is the twenty-one year old version of me. I want to meet him….me."

"But won't that mess up the space-time continuum or whatever it is that they're always going on about in science fiction films? Is that even a thing? You can't meet yourself in time travel?"

"I don't know. Could probably do with messing up if you ask me. Everything else is pretty messed up, or soon will be."

"Do you mean, if you meet him you could change the future; use your influence to stop us all going downhill till we finish up on the edge of World War Three? I don't know what's worse; that or the idea of cannibal cookery shows?"

"Good god, no. I just want him to pick a different girlfriend. My divorce cost me a fortune. The bitch practically bled me dry. Financially, I mean, not.……I just wish I'd thought to make a note of winning lottery numbers as I was growing up."

***

On the train, everything was going smoothly. The passengers were being well looked after by the demon calling herself Maureen, who had declared herself only too happy to stand in for Melanie, as long as she didn't have to wear one of the turquoise uniforms. She just didn't think she had the figure to carry it off. She had to admit that she quite liked humans. The joke that she'd heard her fellow demons make so many times that it wasn't funny, if it ever had been, that she couldn't eat a whole one, was clearly ridiculous. Of course she could! But it wasn't for their flavour that she liked them. They tried so hard and achieved so much, and all without any of the special powers that she wielded. But the humans always seemed to manage to mess things up for themselves. They were so good at hurting each other, there hardly seemed to be a need for the likes of her and her colleague. Still; mustn't grumble. It gives us something to do.

As the train was very crowded and the four musicians were taking up space they hadn't paid for and were being jostled into a corner, Maureen suggested putting the precious guitar in a safe place to protect it. Lloyd gave it up reluctantly, fussing over it as he made sure that it was definitely in a secure place. Maureen led him back to his crowded seat and then continued to check on the welfare of the other people on the train.

She noticed that one of the children is sitting with a Cuddly Satan on her lap. Her dad explains that he got it at a magic shop;

"And here's the funny thing. They didn't have any in stock when I went in, but…."

Maureen interrupts, "Please stop! I know exactly what you're going to say," and she hurries on, away from the sound of him relaying the joke, if that's what he wanted to call it, to another passenger.

An unusual feature of the journey was that all the crossing gates were open in their favour before they reached them. Another unusual feature was the brief stop at the bridge over West Lane in Bledlow, but none of that seemed to spoil the trip, at least for the paying passengers.

When the train returned and the demon walked into the coffee shop, there was still a bit of an atmosphere, Melanie and Jimbo having very different views on things like altruism and ideals.

"Not exactly getting on like a house on fire, eh, if you'll forgive the expression, Melanie."

She gets to her feet; "Not exactly. Bit of a culture clash, as you know. But we'll cope."

"Good! Because it's time to go to work. Some of the passengers are unhappy."

The demons have a quiet word together.

"The looks on those four's faces when they realised what you meant by dropping them off. Priceless."

"Thank you. And I assume the guitar is somewhere safe."

"Of course. Right where you suggested."

No Pleasing Some People

The platform was once again full of people, but this time they were making for the exits, shuffling along slowly, down the ramp to the rail crossing near the signal box and up the stairs to their waiting cars. Most of them dressed in anticipation of the warm sunny weather continuing, as forecast, so there was a lot of grumbling about the way the sky had turned dark, threatening a storm.

Melanie turned to the demon;

"I thought you said you were going to take them up and down the line…..forever."

"Not that lot. They were just the usual ticket holders. They all booked their seats in advance. It didn't feel right to let them down. But not everybody has got off. Listen."

And above the noise of the locomotive hissing and breathing a sigh of relief after its efforts, she could hear somebody shouting and repeatedly working away at door handles that had ceased to function. Even louder shouting and pounding came from the carriage at the back.

"Shall we go and introduce ourselves? I'm not sure these people have any rights, but I'm sure they would like to know why they can't get off." He turns to call to Darryl Clark, who is standing by the engine: "Mister Clark! Put down your shovel; excellent work, I might add; and come and be reunited with your family."

The demon opens the nearest carriage door, and the passengers who had been pressing against it find themselves instead backing away to allow their driver space to climb into the carriage. But they're still puzzled.

"Why couldn't we get this door open? We need to get off. My husband's out there somewhere." Chelsea Clark looks like she's approaching panic attack territory.

"Have no fear, Mrs Clark. Your husband is here; see? He's been making a splendid fist of his footplate experience. Now, while you're all doing your happy reunion stuff, Mr DiRisso, be so good as to hobble along and fetch the two gentlemen who are making that irksome racket in the back of the train."

Darryl is busy trying to brush the worst of the coal dust from his clothes so he can give his wife and daughter a hug. For young Charlie the hugs of childhood have graduated to fist bumps. Cool. The demon herds them fussily into their carriage and the other passengers, sensing that there is only one opening door on the whole train, are starting to clog up the centre aisle.

"Darryl," Chelsea whispers when she can get close enough to her husband. "How did he know I'm your wife? He called me Mrs Clark?"

Darryl thinks his day has been far more baffling than that; he's got to say something though. But before he can put together any kind of answer to whisper back to reassure her, a loud, hectoring voice cuts through the hum of mutterings coming from the confused passengers:

"I insist that you let me off this train. I have a business to run; animals to care for......." Tony Barnes falters as he finds the demon standing right in front of him. Those purple eyes are...are....nobody has purple eyes. Tony bends forward, as the engine driver beckons to him; bends enough for the old man to speak quietly into his ear;

"You're not leaving the train yet. And incidentally, Mr Barnes, I have good reason to believe that your animals are better off without you."

He turns and claps his hands: "Right everybody! Your attention if you please! I'd like you to sit yourselves down on these plush red seats and make yourselves comfortable."

"We can't!"

"What?!"

"We can't get comfortable. These seats are torture. You try and get comfortable on them."

The demon finds his instructions temporarily interrupted by a tall, lean girl in her mid-teens. Defiant: a trouble maker, he thinks.

"Thank you for that observation, Miss Keeley. We'll have to see if we can't find you a cushion at some point; meanwhile you can hear as well standing up, or slouching, or whatever it is that you're doing now."

"How d'you know my name? You been stalking me? You a pervert?"

"That's a very unpleasant accusation. No; I heard your name mentioned by this gentleman here," and he gestures at Gerald, who is being ushered in through the door from the platform. "He was telling me about his family."

"Him? He's not my family. He's just my mum's bloke. She could do a lot better, believe me."

"Keeley!"

"What, Mum?"

"Excuse me." The demon interrupts. "Nobody is interested in your trifling family issues. So please shut up and listen!"

"What did you mean about my animals?"

"How did that arsehole get here?" Gary had followed Gerald into the carriage and clearly, not everyone present was pleased about that.

"Is that man a pirate?"

"STOP!.......Everybody sit, or stand, or slouch; I don't care which. I will explain why you lucky people are here."

"Lucky?"

"Yes, Keeley. Lucky! Your names have been drawn out of the hat for another free ride along the line."

"Lame!"

"You're Charlie, aren't you?"

"How d'you know his name as well? You stalking him too, pervert?"

"No Keeley! I'm not stalking anybody." The demon is beginning to wonder if he's the one being punished.

"Listen, everyone. I realise this may not be the most exciting thing you've ever done, as young Charlie here implied, but you will learn something of compelling interest to each one of you. In the meantime, find yourselves a window to look out of; open carriages here or private compartments in the next carriage. You choose."

"Just one moment! My wife and I paid extra for a private compartment. You can't just let all these......these others into them."

"That's rather mean-spirited of you, Mr Barnes. You've had your money's worth on the first ride. Now this journey is my treat, and I think you will find that I can dictate exactly where people can and can't go. For example, Mr Clark! Give Mr Barnes here your gloves. He's coming to help me turn the engine around.

Barnes' splutterings of indignation are cut short by the raised hand and purple stare.

"So for the rest of you, Mrs Rainham here will be happy to furnish you with tea, coffee or cold drinks, and later as soon as he can get our little canteen into some sort of order, Mr DiRisso will prepare some sandwiches. He is more than adequately qualified to look after your stomachs, I assure you."

He points towards the door and, with a puzzled look at his wife, Barnes collects the gloves from Darryl Clark and leaves the compartment.

"I leave them all in your capable hands, Mrs Rainham. Just carry on as we discussed, and all will be well. And smile. They won't eat you. You're in full control. Understand? Full control."

He leaves, and Melanie braces herself to turn and deliver her best hostess smile. A little wooden, she thinks, both the turn and the smile. *Relax, Melanie.* She takes stock of the varied group of individuals staring back at her. They don't look very relaxed either. There is a general air of discontent among the adults. Ginny Tucker's older two children are oblivious to this as they jump about on the red seats and bang on the tables. Ginny is unconcerned about the noise; she has a crying, wriggling toddler to contend with, while she looks daggers at her former boyfriend.

Charlie didn't hesitate when he heard there were private compartments to be found, but he's none too pleased when he realises Mia is following him.

Annabel Barnes is looking anxiously out of the window, trying to see where her husband has gone. Gerald English pushes himself forward to confront Melanie:

"Never mind tea and coffee. What the fuck is going on? Who does that bloody train driver think he is?"

"I strongly suggest you find a seat, Mr English. And I'll thank you not to use that kind of language with me. (*Where did that come from?*) I don't approve, especially not in front of the children."

Gerald is about to protest, but suddenly finds himself meekly cooperating.

"And kindly stop those children of yours jumping about on the seats!"

"Don't you tell me what to do with my kids, you stuck-up cow!"

"Yeah! Leave our kids be. They're only playing."

Ginny is quite taken aback. That's the first bit of support of any kind she's had from the children's father in ages. But words won't pay her bills, and his actions are worse than useless. At the moment he is backing into a seat, looking, for all the world, intimidated by this uniformed blonde's haughty face. The two lively children climb onto their father's lap and sit quietly.

"That's nice. Now, my name is Melanie. I am your hostess for this journey. We will be setting off again in a few minutes, so can I treat you all to a cup of tea, or coffee? We have crisps and biscuits too, and it's all on the house."

"Ha! Yer mean, s'all on the train, doncha?"

"Yes. Very witty Mr DiRisso. I thought I could hear you clumping up behind me. Do you need something?"

"Not me, nah. Just came ter say wot samwidges we got, 'fennybody wants 'em. Cheese 'n' tom, 'am, choona. Any takers?"

"Is it grated cheese? My three like grated cheese best."

Marvellous; that'll be all over the seats, Melanie thought. *But then why do I care about the seats? I don't even want to be here.*

Jimbo pushed past her.

"Lemme see yer nippers! Oh wot luvverly kids. They's a'most good enough ter eat. Ah cud just gobbl'em all up."

"That's what their Gran says. Sweet enough to eat."

If only you knew what I know, thinks Melanie.

Jimbo turns, and with a wink at Melanie, returns to his makeshift kitchen. "Take some orders, Mrs Rainham," he calls over his shoulder.

"Is that man a pirate?"

"Do you know, young man, I think he probably is. I'll see if I can get him to tell you why he wears an eye patch." *That'll give you nightmares*, she thought. *Your mum, too. Not now! Work to do.*

Melanie gets on with the business of taking orders for refreshments while the train is being gently manoeuvred up and down past the signal box. He seems to have got the hang of this, she thinks. *'Nothing's impossible, for me, Melanie.' Of course….*

She thinks it might be a good idea to find out where everybody is as well. The young mum with the kids, (*Ginny?*) is still in the first carriage, sharing a kind of Mexican Standoff position with (*Gary?*) the man that appears to be the kids' father. He's on the other side of the carriage, close enough to talk, if they want to, and far enough away for them to ignore each other if they don't.

Gerald English and his partner, Bella, are at a table a few rows away. He still looks a bit pensive, probably stunned that a woman had managed to get him to stop complaining and sit down.

Everybody else had moved down to the carriage with the private compartments, only private in the sense that they had windows and a glass-panelled door. Annabel Barnes is sitting with her grandchildren in the first one, looking anxious. She declines the offer of a drink for herself, but the kids go for cartons of fruit juice.

Darryl Clark and his wife and daughter are in the next compartment, Chelsea having bribed Mia with games on her phone to stop her pestering Charlie, who has taken up residence as far away as possible and is showing Keeley something obviously fascinating on his computer. Or perhaps he's just getting to that age where he's fascinated by Keeley.

Back in the food-prep area, where the tea-tray is being loaded up, there is still an uneasy truce between Melanie and Jimbo; at least she finds it uneasy.

"Please don't wind them up with your cannibal references."

"I wasn't. I was winding you up. I've probably worked that to death though. Sorry! I mean, yes; it's got thinnage. So what's the sitch back there? They all seem a bit quiet. They'd be breaking the windows to get out if they knew who their driver was."

"Very quiet, yes. I think he's channelling his power through me while he's out. It's strangely quite satisfying, actually. Well, quiet except for the kids who keep asking if you're a pirate."

"What did you info?"

"I said you probably were. You may have some explaining to do. Jimbo the pirate. What kind of a name is Jimbo?"

"Ah, well my parents named me James, but it's a bit dull for showbiz; very forgettable. Just plain old James Reese from a little place near Oxford."

"Who grew up to be a cannibal…..unbelievable!"

He grins, and goes back to his sandwich prep, humming that old classic, 'I Put a Spell On You."

Melanie isn't listening though. Perhaps it's the demon's control of everybody on the train, everybody including her, that's caused her to overlook something very important to her. But carrying out her hostess duties had preoccupied her to the point where she'd forgotten that one of the passengers was the man who had knocked Greg off his bike.

Home Truths

The powerful little locomotive is an 0-6-0 pannier, the demon informs Tony Barnes, who knew that anyway, but has other things on his mind. It steadily pulls the train of five carriages along the line towards Princes Risborough. Darryl Clark nudges his wife;

"Where is everybody?"

"What do you mean, Hun?"

"Look! There's nobody on the platform. No guards, station master, nobody. Tell a lie; there's the bloke from the coffee bar leaning on the door frame. But nobody with a flag. Did you hear a whistle?"

"Wasn't really listening out for one. What's he like, the driver? Getting on a bit, isn't he? And did you notice his eyes?"

The pace increases a little as they clear the back gardens of Chinnor, not enough to upset anybody's drinks though, and the train settles into a pleasant rhythm for a mile or so, with a deep throaty chug from the engine and the slightly soporific sound of the wheels going over the joins in the rails. At least, they had all thought it was pleasant the first time round, when they'd paid to be there. Now they were reluctant guests who had no idea what their host had in mind for them. He'd said that they were going to learn something of interest, but nobody knew what that meant. Melanie was becoming exasperated with the three young children in the carriage nearest the little kitchen. How could the contents of very small packets of crisps and biscuits cover such a large area? The parents didn't seem to care or even notice, but they had actually started speaking to each other., if you could call "Y'alright?" and "What's it to you?" a conversation.

It's all easy going, slightly downhill, and onwards past the few houses that make up Wainhill, and then the train loses speed, eventually braking to a complete halt alongside the Bledlow Cricket Ground. There is a match in progress, but, with the arrival of the train, the game comes to a halt too. Nobody wants to score a six through a carriage window, and it wasn't unusual for the train to slow or stop here. A smile and a wave is the traditional thing, but today the driver is getting down from the footplate, followed by the fireman. The driver holds a hand up to the sky, and within seconds there is insufficient light to play by. The umpires look at each other, they consult with the players of both teams, they agree that they've never seen the weather change so quickly, and there is a slow, reluctant migration towards the pavilion. Bad light, for sure.

With no platform to level things up, the puzzled faces at the train windows are looking down on the tops of two heads as the demon and Tony Barnes step gingerly along the sleepers, back to the train door which Melanie has opened for them. Barnes pulls himself up first and when they're both inside, the questions start:

"What's happening? Why have we stopped? Who the hell are you anyway?"

"All in good time. Now, have you all been taken care of by your hostess? Plenty to drink?"

"Never mind about the bloody drinks!" Gerald sees himself as the person to sort all this out; he's pushy and people don't tend to argue with him. "I want to know what the fuck is going on?"

He receives the cold purple stare for his interruption.

"I believe Mrs Rainham has already had occasion to speak to you about your use of profanities. Kindly desist!"

"No! I won't! Just who do you think you are? A free ride's all very well, but I only came here to do a delivery. How come my missus and her kid were already here? Some weird bloody coincidence that."

Melanie nudges the demon's arm, "Is it him?" she whispers.

"Not now, Melanie. Later," he snaps at her.

The rising torrent of questions from the other passengers indicates that they have also been thinking about identities and coincidences. From the pocket in the front of his overall, the demon extracts a sheaf of papers, and then a handful of pens. Curiosity reduces the noise level somewhat.

"Before we talk about your questions, I have some for you. We're going to have a brief questionnaire. I would appreciate having your views on certain topics. So take a paper, and a pen. Go back to your seats and employ your thinking abilities, such as they are, for a few minutes to answer the questions. Little Charlie! You too. I think you're old enough to do this."

"Whaddya mean 'little' Charlie? I'm not little."

"No offence intended, young man, but we have Big Charlie back at the station. You might meet him later."

"Whatever. But I'm not little."

"Excuse me. What about our young'uns? They can't do no survey."

"Excellent point, Ms Tucker. Melanie! I'm sure we can find some paper and coloured pencils or crayons for, let me see, six children on board is it? Yes, six."

The Barnes' granddaughter, who looks to be about seven years old, asks what they should draw. Her slightly older brother says,

"Can I draw the pirate?"

"Yeah! An' I wanna draw the engine driver."

"Very flattering, Alice. And your brother's Arran, yes? I'm sure Mr DiRisso would be happy to pose for you."

"If you know so much about us already, and God knows how, why do we have to fill in this thing?"

"An excellent question again, Mr Barnes. But I'm keen to canvass your views on certain subjects. Once I have those, it will be a lot clearer to you why you're all here. So! Off you trot; start writing. Melanie! Paper and crayons for the children."

Once again, the passengers find themselves complying with the driver's commands, no matter how much it goes against their natural inclination. Tony and Annabel Barnes look at each other across their table.

"Did you manage alright in the engine, love?"

"Yes, fine. Fine. Just not used to all that shovelling…. I have to say these are very strange questions. I was expecting something about our railway journey. I've got some very strong views on that I can tell you."

"I see what you mean."

Question One
It's the first day of your holiday on the Costa del Sol. You open the blinds of your hotel room window to find that your view is obscured by abandoned fridges, bin bags and pieces of polystyrene.
Do you:
   a)   Complain to the management?
   b)   Decide to rate them low on Tripadvisor?
   c)   Enjoy the view?

Question Two
While out driving you come across a Roe Deer that has just been knocked over by a car and is in obvious distress.
Do you:
   a)   Stop to see if you can help?
   b)   Phone an animal rescue centre?
   c)   Drive on because it's only a deer?

Question Three
You're walking your children to school and a car comes past at well over 30 mph, narrowly missing your family.
Do you:
   a)   Shout abuse at the driver?
   b)   Make a note of the registration number?
   c)   Applaud his excellent car control?

Question Four

Social media platforms, such as Facebook, are excellent for:

a) Keeping in touch with friends.
b) Sharing community information.
c) Saying things you wouldn't dare to speak.

"How are you all getting on with my questions? Not too difficult I hope."

"Don't see what you're getting at, mate. Is this some kind of a joke?"

"No, Mr English. It's not a joke, and I'm not very surprised that you, of all people, don't see, as you put it, what I'm getting at."

"What's that supposed to mean?"

"Explaining that to you would take more time than I want to invest. And one other thing, Mr English; I'm not your mate. Right everybody!! There's a second set of questions. They're a little more personal. Enjoy…."

Question Five

You have been paid to dispose of some rubbish from a home improvement project.

Do you:

a) Take the materials to a waste disposal site?
b) Dump the rubbish in a layby?

Question Six

You are the owner of a sick animal. You have lots of animals to look after.

Do you:

a) Call a vet to help the animal?
b) Ignore the problem and let it die in pain?

Question Seven

You are offered a truck driving job, for cash. You have no licence to drive the truck or insurance.

Do you:

a)   Decline the offer because it would be illegal?
b)   Pocket the tax-free cash and drive anyway?

Question Eight

You see a new post on Facebook which mentions that a cyclist has been knocked off their bike and sustained serious injuries.

Do you:

a)   Join in with the expressions of sympathy?
b)   Say it was probably their own fault?

"What the hell is this all about, you bastard?"

"Your language, Mr English! Please! Last question was a bit difficult for you, was it? I'm guessing that some of you would have only managed three out of four answers at best. So let's have everybody in the same room. Leave the children doing their pictures, and we'll talk about why you're all here, shall we?"

"I'm not leaving my kids here with that pirate. Can't you just say your piece here? No offence."

"Wotta pity. Ah was gonna make 'em all walk the plank when you was out."

"As you wish, Ms Tucker. If everybody could find somewhere to sit we will say something about these questionnaires. It's interesting, although completely predictable, that only two people managed to answer all the questions; the youngest members of your group. Now I wonder why that is. Anybody?"

"They were pretty bloody strange questions for a train ride if you ask me. So if you got summat to say, out with it."

"As you wish Mr English. I'll come to the point then. You are all here because somebody thinks you deserve to be punished."

The demon allows a little time for the responses to die down.

"Yes, I thought that would cause a reaction."

"But I ain't done nothing!"

"You say that, Mr English, although your abuse of the English language alone merits punishment in my opinion; rather ironic, that. But actually, it's your actions that are chiefly responsible for us all being here on this train together."

"That's ridiculous. I think you're....absurd."

"Really? We'll address that viewpoint later. But for now, we're going to run through the questions I posed for you. On second thoughts; dearie me. I'm forgetting my manners. None of you have been formally introduced, have you?"

"I don't give a shit about knowing who these people are. I want to get off this bloody train!"

"Ah, but you can't, Mr English."

"Who says I can't? Little runt like you isn't gonna stop me. And how come you know so much about us, eh?"

"That's a fair question, and I must apologise for putting you all at a disadvantage. Perhaps I should explain who I am. Young Alice there knows who I am, don't you, Alice?"

All heads turn to look at the Barnes' granddaughter, who is looking very shaken and tearful.

"Would you like to show everybody what you've drawn, Alice? Don't be shy. It's a very good picture. You should be proud of it."

Alice hands the piece of paper to her grandfather, who unfolds it and then holds it up for the others.

"Is this some kind of a joke? That looks like the Incredible Hulk."

"Oh, bigger than that, Mr Barnes. And notice all the teeth and claws. She's got me to a T."

"Why did you draw that, Alice? It's horrible," her Gran asks, putting an arm round the now sobbing child.

"Because he's a monster."

"Rubbish!"

But before Gerald can reach the door he was inching towards, the whole atmosphere changes. The carriage is plunged into the deepest black, interrupted every few seconds by intense flashes of light. In those few illuminated moments the screaming, panicking passengers are treated to a real life version of Alice's picture, a creature that seems to fill one end of the carriage from floor to ceiling. A tremendous rumbling noise and vibration runs through the train, the darkness clears, and the few people who aren't cowering on the floor realise that the train has started moving, travelling at a speed it was certainly never designed for. And then suddenly, everything is calm again, apart from the sobbing, coughing, wheezing and swearing noises coming from the terrified people who have just been through the most astonishing experience of their lives.

The demon is back to his guise as their driver, a slight smirk on his wrinkled old face as he waits for calm. Gerald English, though, persists in his attempts to escape, tries to run to the other end of the carriage, where his path is blocked by another monstrous figure. He falls to his knees in terror.

"Ah, Maureen. Time to get changed, I think, and help Mr English back to his seat. We don't need to overdo it now, do we?"

Gary, the van driver, points at Melanie.

"Is she like that too?"

"No, Mr Fotherby. She's like you: human. And, like you, she's here to be punished. Feel free to chat with her if you still have any doubts about what I'm capable of."

"And him. What about the pirate?"

"Oh, Mr DiRisso? I hate to disappoint the kiddies, but he's not a real pirate. But he is a real cannibal."

"That was cool, Mister! Do it again!"

Let's Take A Vote

"Ridiculous, I think, was the word you used, Mr English. Still want to go with that? Cat got your tongue?"

"Hurr! Ah hope it ain't. Ah'll hafter change tonight's menu."

"Very witty, Mr DiRisso. Kindly desist while I enlighten our guests."

Annabel Barnes interrupts, "Please, whoever you are. We'll give you anything. We just want to go home. What have we done to deserve this?"

"Mrs Barnes. You will go home when, or possibly even if, I've finished with you and not before. As I've already told you, you're here to be punished."

"Punished for what? At least let the children go! What have they done, for pity's sake?"

"Ah yes. The children. They have so much to learn, don't they? And you probably think that you're the best ones to teach them. Right now I need you all to take a seat and listen to me. Melanie here will bring you drinks if you require them; tea, coffee, water, something stronger, perhaps. A glass of port, Mrs Barnes? Your usual? No?

Later perhaps, then?"

Reaching once again into the front pocket of his overalls, the demon extracts a document folder. He opens it and extracts a sheet of paper.

"Before I start introducing a little clarity as to why each of you have earned a seat on my train, I'll explain who I am. You've seen what I look like, and you've seen my colleague, the one who answers to 'Maureen'. I am here in answer to a number of distress calls, from your fellow humans who are so disgusted by your behaviour that they have called down evil upon you, or they have turned to some form of what they believe is magic in a desperate attempt to get back at you. I am sometimes referred to as a vengeance demon. So there you are; that's me. Now let's talk about you."

"Wait a minute! What do you mean, disgusted by our behaviour? How dare you!"

"Yeah! And why are the children here? What have they done?"

"Well you couldn't very well leave them at home on their own, could you? Although I read here, Ms Tucker, that you do sometimes have occasion to do that when you need some 'me time', as you call it."

Gary Fotherby snaps to attention at this and turns on his ex.

"What? You useless bitch! You leave my kids home alone?"

"Sit down, Mr Fotherby! Ms Tucker! Quiet! Interestingly, one of my clients made a comment that I jotted down. Let's see; 'These people shouldn't be allowed to breed'. That was said of you, Mr Clark."

"That's outrageous. Who would say such a thing? We've got two lovely children."

"Indeed you have. Young, but not 'Little'," he added hastily, "Charlie, and sweet little Mia. I wonder how long they'll stay lovely with you as their father. Don't get me wrong, I have nothing but admiration for your skill at shovelling coal, but other aspects of your life merit question."

He reaches up to put a hand on Darryl's shoulder and turns him to face the audience.

"Permit me to introduce to you Mr Darryl Clark. May we call you Darryl?.... Good. Darryl struggled a bit with Question Five on our quiz. You see, Darryl is a fly-tipper, one of those people that is paid good money to dispose of rubbish, promises faithfully and with a cheery smile that he will take it to the proper facility, but instead, finds a quiet spot in the countryside to dump it and thus avoids any of those irritating legally required fees. And you'll all be glad to know that Darryl doesn't waste his money. He has a beautiful aquarium full of very expensive tropical fish."

"How do you know that?"

"Silly question, Darryl. I realise you haven't known me for long, but really! One of my client's other comments was that people like Darryl have no place in decent society. What do you all think, eh? You're certainly out of decent society now, Darryl."

"What do you mean? Are you saying we're not decent people? My husband and I run a very successful business.

We're nothing like that man."

"Indeed you do, Mrs Barnes. Annabel?.... Yes, good. Well it used to be a very successful business. Some of you have probably been to the adventure farm and petting zoo that the Barnses run on the north side of Oxford. Yes, I thought so. You've been, haven't you Maureen?"

"Oh yes! I particularly liked the chickens."

"I bet you did, but I doubt that your visit did the profit and loss sheet much good. A drop in the ocean, though. Anyway, as I was saying, it used to be a successful business until that whole coronavirus experience came along and closed everything down. Your bank account has been haemorrhaging money, hasn't it Tony? All those buildings to maintain, animals to feed, staff to pay, and Annabel still tripping off to London in the Range Rover to meet her friends for lunch and a matinée. Not easy, is it Tony?"

"No, but you have no right to discuss my personal affairs in front of all these people."

"I suppose we could talk about rights, Tony; animal rights specifically. My colleague, Maureen, was contacted by a lady and her group of friends and apparently the lady had already informed you that one of your horses was extremely ill. Your hostile response to her and continued neglect resulted in the animal suffering pain for several days, until a veterinarian arrived to end its misery. Inexcusable, the lady said. She obviously didn't know about your financial worries, but even if she had, I think she would still have said it was inexcusable. What do the rest of you think?"

"Disgusting. People like him shouldn't be allowed to keep animals."

"Indeed, Mr English. That's what Maureen's client said. Funny; I anticipated that you would be the first one to express an opinion."

"What's that supposed to mean?"

"All in good time, Gerald. Meanwhile, Tony, let's look for the positives here. You're beyond the reach of any legal proceedings at the moment, and for some time to come. Talking of legal proceedings, we turn our attention now to Mr Gary Fotherby, Gaz to his friends. Do you feel like you're among friends here, Gary? You and Ms Tucker seem to be completely at odds just lately."

"That's because he's a useless piece of shit who never gives me any money for his kids."

"Look, I'm going to leave you in Maureen's capable hands. She will supervise your analysis of those honeyed words, but at this moment I need to have a quiet word with Melanie before we go any further."

He leads Melanie through the connection into the next carriage and takes her as far out of earshot of the others as he can. Melanie is shaking with anger.

"It's him, isn't it? The van driver."

"Yes, of course it's him. It didn't take a genius to work that out. The question is, what are we going to do about him? Or more specifically, what are you going to do about him?"

"You want me to do something about him? Is that what you're saying?"

"On the contrary. I mean I don't object if you spill the occasional hot cup of tea on him; accidents happen. But restrain yourself from any other vengeful activities. That's my job. Remember what happened last time you defied me? The chair?"

"But he's such a scumbag. Did you hear the way he spoke to his girlfriend or whatever she is? Like he actually had some standards?"

"Indeed. He's a very troubled young man. But, this is interesting. Your daughter did a sort of buy-one-get-one-free deal. That's how come we've got the excruciating Gerald English on board. You'll have noticed how free with his opinions he is."

"Interesting? You say that like it's some kind of social experiment. I'd just like to get my hands on that van driver.. That would be interesting."

"You will do no such thing. But I have plans for both him and for Mr English, that neither of them will like very much. So we're going back to join the others, you are going to restrain yourself, and we will continue with the introductions, yes?"

"I don't really have a choice, do I? Nobody does with you, do they?"

"In a nutshell. Come on. Back to work. I suspect that there has been some hostility developing while we've been through here."

On their return to the next carriage they discover a distressed Ginny Tucker being comforted by Chelsea Clark, while Gary Fotherby is thwarted in his attempts to approach her by a wall made up of Darryl Clark and

Gerald English. Maureen has Ginny's three children sitting with her, one on her lap and the other two pressed up against her on the seat, as she reads them a story. She looks up:

"I know. It's not really me, is it? But these little chickadees are so cute."

"Perhaps. Can't see it myself, but just remember that they're chickadees, not chickens. I see you have everything under control." He nods to the two tense groups at opposite ends of the room.

"Oh they didn't need me. It's good to see them getting to know one another, don't you agree? And I think they're a little wary of me getting involved in their disputes for some reason."

The demon claps his hands. The sound overrides all the conversation and crying, and focuses everybody's attention.

"Now, if you recall, we were just about to introduce Mr Gary Fotherby. I see some of you are getting acquainted already, although not quite at the 'Gaz' stage yet. Mr Fotherby has developed irresponsibility to a fine art. I'm sure most of you will have worked out his relationship with Ms Tucker, and have heard her complaints. His dereliction of paternal duty is just the tip of the iceberg, isn't it Gary?"

"Up yours, ya creep!"

"Somehow I don't imagine that's ever going to happen, but brave words, Gary. Bravo! Bet you're all dying to know what Gary's here for. Takes the heat off the fly-tipper and the horse-killer a bit. Gary is a van driver; one of your beloved 'white-van-men'. Sometimes he's a lorry driver.

You probably saw him loading supplies onto the train earlier, and for that we thank you, Gary. We may be justified, however, in taking issue with Gary's complete absence of a valid driving licence, or any insurance, or any intention of paying tax on the money he earns."

"Lots of people do cash in hand jobs. Why pick on me?"

"I believe you're right, Gary. But not so many people drive a truck along busy roads when they've been, I believe you would say, getting stoned until four in the morning. Do you remember that, Gary? About three years ago, wasn't it? There you are, no licence, no insurance, no consideration for the consequences if you had an accident."

"That's none of your business. I got fined for that, an' I paid it."

"But you were banned from driving, and here you are today, with another van."

"Well that bloke on the bike shoulda looked where he was going? Can't blame me for that?"

"It seems the magistrates took a different view, though, so legally, you haven't got a leg to stand on, which is an unfortunate expression, because neither has your victim. The gentleman on the bike has been in a wheelchair ever since."

"Look, I'm sorry about that, but how was I to know he was gonna turn right. I'm not a friggin' mind reader."

"We'll possibly all have a think about your impaired ability to make reasonable anticipations later, but at this point I would like to introduce you all to Mr Gerald English. Say hello to everybody, Gerald."

Gerald just nods, looking uncomfortable, wondering what's in store for him.

"Just as you wish, Gerald. I believe you share Gary's views on who was to blame for the accident."

"I don't know what you're on about. And I have no idea why you've got me lumped in with this lot."

The demon reaches in his folder for another piece of paper.

"Hmm. You do seem to have a somewhat ungracious attitude to your fellow travellers, don't you? Here's the transcript of a conversation that you contributed to online, a Facebook conversation on the subject of cyclists. You don't like cyclists, do you, Gerald? A young lady commented that her father had been knocked off his bike and was now paralysed. Is everybody beginning to see the connection here? Good. So quick as a flash, Gerald joins in with, "He should of looked where he was going then". The sensitive among you may find it hard to overlook his appalling grammar; I certainly can't. But the young lady who received this reply was outraged, and, to cut a long story short, she contacted me."

"Well I'm very sorry about all that, but…."

"But what, Gerald? You're a media troll. A cowardly keyboard warrior. Never stop to think about how your bigoted opinions affect people, and with that opinion, you upset the wrong person."

"So I get all this crap for expressing my opinions?"

"Well for years you've just been kicked off one Facebook group after another, because people are sick of your 'opinions', but I think this is much more inventive, don't you? And you'll be staying off Facebook for a while too, so it's win-win for the general public I'd say."

"What do you mean by a while? What are you going to do with us?"

"Glad you asked me that. One of the regular events on this railway is a Murder Mystery evening, dinner included. So I thought we'd do that. Sounds fun?"

"We can't be here all evening. I need to feed my tropical fish. They cost a fortune," Darryl Clark complains.

"Don't you worry about them. Leave that to me. What I need you all to do is take a little time to think about this. I want you to select which one of you is going to be the murder victim: the fly-tipper, the horse-killer, the truck driver or the internet troll."

"You surely don't really mean…. murder? For real?"

"You better believe it, Tony. And just one more thing, specifically for Gary and Gerald: thought I'd better let you know this….. Melanie, your charming hostess, gets a vote too. She is the unfortunate cyclist's wife. Good luck, gentlemen. Let's take a vote!"

Democracy off the Rails

"You can't seriously expect us to vote to have somebody killed. This is monstrous."

"Is it, Mr Barnes? Although, as your granddaughter pointed out to you all, I am a monster. Isn't that what she said?"

"Well we refuse to vote. We don't execute people for petty crimes in this country. Any crimes, come to that. So you can play your twisted game without me and my wife, thank you very much."

"You raise one interesting point there, Mr Barnes, and it's good to see you suddenly remembering the laws of 'this country'. But you're not in good old Blighty anymore. You're all on my train and I am your supreme ruler; a dictator, if you like. Or if you don't like."

"No, I don't like it."

"You don't have to like dictators, Mr Barnes. You just have to do what they dictate. Hence the word. It's not a democracy. And right now I'm dictating that you vote for a victim. Although I suppose that is democracy. I'm confusing you all. And myself! No matter! I've provided you with this lovely ballot box; look! There you are; our first slogan for this thrilling new game: Vote For A Victim!"

"I'm with Barnes. I'm not voting either."

"Aren't you, Mr English? That's a pity. Anybody else?.....I see. My first decree and I find mass rebellion. Does nobody want to participate?"

"I do." Melanie steps forward and very theatrically inserts a folded piece of paper into the ballot box, staring hard at Gary Fotherby the whole time, dispelling any doubt as to which way she was voting. The gesture provokes Ginny Tucker.

"Who's that stuck-up cow looking at? You're not killing my Gary. These kids need a father."

Gary Fotherby looks round in surprise, his front-running in the Victim Stakes momentarily forgotten. The demon smiles.

"Well isn't this nice? Melanie, I do believe you've acted as a sort of a catalyst. Excellent. Now, about this voting procedure. There's no rush. I suppose you could call me a benevolent dictator. For now. We'll just keep chugging up and down the line until the votes are in. I've got all the time in the world."

"I thought you said we were having a Murder Mystery Night tonight."

"No, Mr English. I didn't say it would be tonight. Like I said, all the time in the world. Take as long as you like. Obviously, if you all abstain I'll just have to accept the one vote that's in the box. Think about it. So! Mr Clark. I require your skill with the shovel. It's time to get moving again."

The engine driver and his fireman leave the carriage and the hubbub of noise that ensues takes the trio that comprise the crew some considerable time and patience to decipher into something like intelligible speech. Words like 'children' and 'cannibal' and 'collaborator' are just about identifiable through the babble, suggesting a whole range of viewpoints will require dealing with. But when the words beginning with 'c' become shorter, blunter and altogether more offensive, Maureen decides to call a halt to the conversation.

Once everybody's ears have recovered from her intervention she speaks;

"Mr Fotherby! I sense a little animosity towards our Melanie here. I can understand that, but kindly moderate your language."

"You what? She's quite happy to vote for me to get murdered and you complain about how I talk. I said I was sorry, didn't I?"

"Oh well that makes all the difference. Does that seem fair to you, Melanie?"

"My vote stands. The world's better off without him."

"There you go, Gary dear. The world's better off without you. You should be proud of the opportunity to make the world a better place. Now stop being such a baby, and keep your opinions to yourself. It appears other people have questions. Annabel, dear. You're usually very quiet. What do you want to say?"

"Thank you. I mean, how long do you think you can get away with this? People will notice we're missing, won't they? And what about the train people? You can't just keep running their train up and down."

"Yeah! They'll 'ave the police on yer."

"Your friends, the police. Do shut up, Gary. No, they won't come, and here's why. What day is it today? Anybody?"

"Sunday."

"Thank you, Gerald. And what day is it tomorrow?"

"Monday, obviously."

"Well done. Monday. And the day after that?"

It should be obvious, but they can see this brewing up to being a trick question.

"Nobody? I'll tell you then. Monday. You've heard the expression 'a month of Sundays'? To borrow another line, 'you ain't seen nuthin' yet'."

The barrage of noise that followed Maureen's statement reached new peaks of volume, but this time, along with the anger, there were tears, adult tears, which set the children off. Tony Barnes detached himself, as well as he could, from the very audible chaos and placed himself directly in front of Maureen.

"This is inhuman. You can't keep us all here."

"I think you've hit the nail on the head there, Tony. Inhuman! I'm not human. The driver's not human. You have no idea of the power we have. The person driving this train has hijacked the railway line, but nobody out there can see it. They're unable to see it, we've seen to that. And anyway, the train never runs on a Monday. So we're just going to keep repeating Monday."

"I don't get it. What do you mean, repeating Monday? Do you mean like that film, Groundhog Day?"

"Yes, Chelsea; Ooh, I saw that the other night. Isn't it good?…. Well I thought so…. But here's the thing; it'll be the same Monday outside all the time you're here, but time will move on as normal on the train."

"How is that possible?"

"I have absolutely no idea, to tell you the truth. Derek does all that stuff, I don't. But look on the bright side. If you were due to go back to work on Monday morning, you'll miss it. No chance of being stuck in traffic here."

But Tony Barnes has a defiant look on his face;

"You can't keep us here overnight. Somebody will come looking for us. My grandchildren should have gone back to their parents on Sunday evening. If we don't turn up, they'll wonder where we are. In fact, I'll phone them now."

He reaches for his phone and young Charlie speaks up;

"It probably isn't working, Mister. Mine isn't. Can't get Tiktok, Instagram, Facebook, Twitter; nothing."

As everybody checks their phones, only to confirm that what Charlie had just said was true, Maureen spoils Tony's hope of escape.

"I'm sure the rest of your family will be more than welcome to join us if they show up. You and your son can sit and chat about animal welfare together. And I'm sure we can cater for two more. Plenty of food to go round, Mr DiRisso?"

"There's plenty thanks, Mo. Fennyboddy's feeling 'ungry, just gimme a wink. I'd wink back, but it all goes dark when I do that."

"What's this about you being a cannibal?" Chelsea asks. "I don't want a cannibal feeding my kids."

"Praps that was a bit ofan exaggeration. I never actually ett people. I've cooked plenty, mind. An' I spose, like most cooks, yer 'avter taste what yer've made, doncha?"

This met with stunned silence and looks ranging from disbelief to revulsion. Maureen interrupts:

"Thank you, Jimbo. But that's all in the past. No actually, it's all in the future. Never mind; it's complicated. The point is, James is a very good chef, and I'm sure he can cater to all your dietary requirements, although given that we've only got a couple of camping stoves on board, he's going to have his work cut out. Any more questions before I hand you over to Melanie here, who I'm sure will be only too happy to take orders for food or drink?"

I don't feel very happy, thought Melanie.

"She doesn't look very happy to me," said Gerald. "If she's not a monster like you, how come she's working for you? Don't seem right to me. That's collaborating with the enemy, that's what that is."

Melanie decided it might be time to step up to her rôle

as Customer Services manager. The demon had said he'd only let her go if she turned in an adequate performance, so….perform.

"Mr English," she said quietly so that he had to draw close to hear her. "I think we're all having a very challenging day and I, for one, would rather be doing other things. But it seems unlikely that we'll be getting off any time soon, and do you know? I've earmarked you as a bit of an influencer. I'm sure if the others see you ordering a drink or a sandwich they'll see sense and follow suit." *Flatter the bastard. Mess with his head.*

"What? Too right I don't wanna be here, but I suppose you're right. Need to keep my strength up if there's any chance of escaping." *There isn't. No chance.* "Got any bottled beers, and maybe a ham sarnie?"

"And perhaps your good lady would like something too?"

Gradually, the majority of the occupants of the carriage put in orders for refreshments. Melanie wonders how much of it was Gerald who set the ball rolling, or whether there was some other influence that was making them so compliant.

While this was going on, the train had reached Princes Risborough, an event which had caused no reaction whatsoever from anybody waiting for trains on the mainline platforms. Steam trains usually provoke smiling and waving, but this time: nothing at all. It was just as Maureen had told them; nobody could see them. For the second time that day, the passengers commenced their return journey. Melanie knew that it wouldn't be their last.

Jimbo DiRisso was busy turning out sandwiches,

113

pasties and cakes to fill the orders that Melanie brought in. He was looking at her curiously and she sensed he was keen to talk. No doubt the revelation about her husband's cycling accident had sparked his interest. It occurred to Melanie that, investigative journalist or nosey parker he claimed to be, and even though they hadn't got off to a very good start, he was at least somebody to talk to; somebody human and not demon. She would proceed with caution. Human he may be, but one that was very difficult to trust, to feel completely at ease with.

The train pulled up to the platform at Chinnor and stopped. Gary Fotherby jumped up to try a door handle, and the door opened, but only to let in the driver and Darryl Clark.

"Mr Fotherby! Your enthusiasm does you credit. Excellent timing. Mr Clark could do with a break from his duties on the footplate, so you can come and do the next stint."

"We're going round again?"

"You catch on eventually, don't you, Gary. Yes, we're going round again. By the time I've finished with you, you'll know every leaf and blade of grass by name. You'll be on speaking terms with the rabbits and the pheasants, which in your case is probably a good result; nobody else has much time for you."

"Do you have to be so rude?"

"Ah, Ms Tucker! Y'know, I do believe there's a glimmer of hope for you there, Gary. Now come on! We have an engine to turn round. Oh," he adds, turning in the doorway. "How's the voting coming on?"

114

He shepherds Gary through the door, leaving the passengers unsettled again. Most of them had been trying to ignore the ballot papers. It was a welcome distraction for them to question Darryl about his experience at the front of the train.

"No, he didn't hurt me," he says in answer to his wife. "When he's out there he's just a dead enthusiastic old railway nut. Never stopped talking about how the thing works. I'd be learning loads if I wasn't trying to think of a way out of this."

Maureen reaches out and takes him by the hand.

"There isn't a way out, dear, so come and sit down with your family. Melanie will bring you a beer and a snack, I'm sure. And we'll be off again in a couple of minutes. I do believe our host has a special treat for you, Darryl."

"I don't like the sound of that. What have I done now?"

"Don't worry, dear. It's just something he thought you might appreciate."

She refuses to be drawn into answering any more questions, and presently the train starts its next journey east. Darryl takes Chelsea and Mia to a private compartment for a bit of peace and quiet. Charlie is off with Keeley somewhere, playing games on his i-pad and her phone, offline, and wondering if there are any charging points anywhere on this ancient relic of a train.

Ginny Tucker is looking for somewhere quiet too; the baby's nappy needs changing. She has delegated her supervision of the other two to their dad, muttering as she passes that he's changing the next one. Not exactly a peace treaty, but it's the closest they've got to mutual cooperation for months.

Tony and Annabel Barnes have also taken themselves off to a private compartment, the one that Tony thinks of as his, because he has a ticket to say it is. He's sitting perusing the various bits of paper that the driver gave them: the two quiz sheets, with their strange, incisive questions, and the ballot paper for this preposterous Murder Mystery idea. The feller couldn't seriously mean one of them was going to die.

Gerald English was trying to console Bella, assuring her that he would find a way to get them off this train. "They can't keep decent people imprisoned like this." His confident words didn't match the turbulent mental activity he had going on, as he realised that he had nothing to go up against the power that the driver and this Maureen character had displayed. Maybe he could work on that hostess woman; Melanie, wasn't it? She'd picked him to talk to earlier. Perhaps she sensed his leadership qualities. God knows, nobody else seemed to be stepping up to the plate. Maybe she had some influence with these freaks. He'd have to tread warily though. Didn't they say something about this woman's daughter being the one who'd landed him here in the first place? That was nonsense. He'd been delivering vegetables to the railway station. On a bicycle. Although, come to think, that was just as nonsensical.

His attempts to make sense of this were suddenly interrupted by a child shouting from further up the train.

"Look, Daddy! There's a man sitting on a sofa!"

Like everybody else, Gerald looked to see what young Mia was shouting about. By the side of the track, smiling and waving, there was indeed somebody sitting on a sofa. It was the demon engine-driver. As the train chugged slowly forwards, the passengers found their view obscured by piles of rubbish: fridges, cardboard boxes, black sacks with their contents spilling out and spreading into the fields and gardens, long defunct television sets, all interspersed with dilapidated sofas; on each one, the driver sitting, smiling and waving.

Darryl feels a hand on his shoulder. It's Maureen. She whispers,

"There you are, dear. I said there would be a special treat for you. There's the countryside, just the way you like it."

Supply Shortages

"I can't wait to see what he's got in store for the dead-horse chappie."

"Jimbo! I didn't hear you coming." Melanie almost knocks over the used plates she was stacking to clear away. She regains her balance and takes them through to the small kitchen area. Jimbo follows her.

"Good! I'm getting down with this leg at last. They're far uber at prosthetics when I come from. It just takes a while to get used to shoe weight."

"I hope I never have to find out. You seem pretty philosophical about whatever happened to you. It turns my stomach just thinking about it."

"Now I've had time to get away from 'then', so to speak, I agree with you; sick, in the old sense of the word. We just became desensitised to an increasingly violent world, and some very violent entertainment. Where we are now, these are the Good Old Days. I guess every generation does that. When I was young, people would talk about the Good Old Days of the nineteen seventies, and the people who grew up in the fifties moaned about the debauchery of long-haired rock stars, IRA bombers, striking dockers and miners. Copy that?"

"I know exactly what you're saying, although I shudder to think how anybody will look back upon 2050 and call that the Good Old Days. But right now, I would think if you asked any of the passengers, they would say any day before they got on this train was much better than now. I'm worried about what's going to happen to them."

"Worried? And I'm thinking you're the Ice Queen. Surely you're not worried about that van driving fool, are you? Guessing he was the one that got your vote earlier."

"No, I'm not bothered about him. It's just…..how are they all going to start behaving after a few days of being cooped up here? I'm not sure how I'm going to cope, to be honest. I've had enough of being imprisoned by that demon."

Jimbo pauses for a second or two, looking thoughtful.

"Look, Melanie…..down with me calling you Melanie? Okay. Look, I know we didn't get down good up front. I was totes rude, chauvy and all that. It was the showman coming out, and I sometimes forget to switch it off. So please, I give you my humbles."

"Apology accepted, if that's what you mean, although I hope you're not just worming your way in to get a good story."

"Not professionally, no. Although I'm always keen to hear good goss. But no; I'm with you. I think we've got a bit of a powder-keg situation here. I mean, I'm sure it's all very larky for our demonic host, and he makes a totally good case for doing down the guilty, but most of the people on board haven't actually done anything. A bit harsh."

"He has very imaginative ways of punishing people, believe me. But how come you're here? You must be the only human on board that isn't a prisoner. Why did he rescue you and not just leave you to face the music?"

"You say I'm not a prisoner not so sure, me. But I can't figure that one out either. He didn't owe me anything and he had no reason to feel sorry for me. I'd dished up enough misery myself, pardon my pun."

"I've been trying to put that image out of my head. Thanks!"

"Sorry. But do you mind if I ask? You hint at something that's happened to you, apart from landing this plum job obviously."

Melanie decides that it can't hurt to tell him that, at least. She had been thinking about telling him something about her experiences anyway; an intelligent human to talk to.

"The plum job, as you call it, was the only alternative to what he'd had me doing before."

"Which was?"

"Sitting in a chair for four years."

"What!? You're kidding…..you're not kidding. That's just appalling."

"Isn't it? On the plus side, I was in some sort of coma for most of the time, so I would only wake up and scream every now and again. And then he tells me that my husband's been paralysed by that bastard Fotherby, and my family all think I'm dead."

"Good grief, Woman. You've been milled, totally. Hell did you do to deserve that? Was it the arson and the cat poisoning he was talking about?"

"Well, yes and no. The details aren't important. I don't want to talk about that. Not yet. It was more that he said I'd broken the rules."

"Rules?"

"His rules. Look, I asked him to do a job for me. He took twenty seven bloody years to get around to it, and then didn't do it very well. Not in my opinion anyway. So I tried to do it myself, and he got all shirty about that. I broke the rules; so four years in the chair. He let me out because of his bloody steam train obsession. Needed me to be a trolley dolly, is what he told me. Or Head of Customer Services, is how he glammed it up."

At that point, Maureen pokes her head through the door. She'd clearly been listening to their conversation.

"The Head of Customer Services is just who we need right now. People are complaining that they're getting bored. I think the novelty of the track-side rubbish show wore off after about three miles. Darryl's looking a touch subdued. I think he's worried that it might have influenced the voting. So, any ideas?"

Melanie and Jimbo look at each other, seeking inspiration. He shrugs. Melanie hadn't really thought very far beyond the original trolley dolly brief.

"Is there anything on this old rattle trap we can entertain them with? I can't just keep offering them tea and crisps."

"Nah! They won't want their dinnaz!"

"Stop it, Jimbo!" Both Melanie and Maureen have had enough of that voice. "Seriously. Even a box of board games would help."

"You think? You've all been taken prisoner by a demon train driver. Anybody fancy a game of Scrabble? They're not really in the mood for that."

"The littl'uns have nodded off and the other kids are either looking out of the window or playing on phones. I fear the worst when the batteries run out."

"Thanks, Maureen. Can't you use your power to recharge them? It might prevent a riot."

"I don't hold with riots. I always seem to get lumbered with tidying up afterwards. So I reckon I could charge the phones and whatnot. And if we dig out a few jigsaw puzzles from that cupboard over there, although what's the betting they're all pictures of trains?, give them some more paper to scribble on, that might help. Might….. You keep chatting up Gerald and plying him with drink….."

"Excuse me! I was not chatting him up!"

"Well whatever you were doing, he's started speaking very highly of you. Thinks you're probably an astute judge of character."

"The slimy bastard's probably just trying to make sure I don't decide to change my vote. I wouldn't chat him up if he was the last man on the planet."

"Or on the train. Let me know if you manage to arrange them into some sort of order, won't you? But whatever it is that you're doing, it's keeping him sweet for now. I think the women with the young kids could be trouble though; a touch of the tigress defending its cubs," says Maureen. "Nothing we can't handle. Do you know what? I've discovered that I actually quite like entertaining the little perishers, but there are only so many Thomas the Tank Engine books you can read before you glaze over."

The passengers aren't saying much. They don't look very cheerful, but they're not saying or doing very much, except Gerald, who is still optimistically trying all the door handles.

"Planning to jump are you, Gerald? We must be doing at least fifteen miles per hour. A fall at that speed could be fatal."

He snaps back angrily at Maureen; "Somebody has to make an effort to get away from you freaks. I'm not one for sitting around doing nothing."

"True. You're more into sitting around hammering out libellous nonsense on your computer keyboard."

"Now look here…I don't have to put up with all this abuse."

"But other people do, yes? Here's an idea, Gerald. I'm sure if you ask your lovely friend Melanie, really nicely, she'll give you some paper and a pen. Why don't you sit and write some sort of a journal. Tell the world all about our experiences together. And if you struggle with the spelling or grammar, I'm sure Mr DiRisso here would be happy to help you, wouldn't you, Jimbo?"

"Urr! That I might."

"What use would that one-eyed freak be?"

"Oh dear. Is that another one of your prejudices, Gerald? First cyclists; now the disabled. Tut tut….. It turns out that Mr DiRisso is a very well qualified writer; Oxford graduate and all that. But I see we're pulling into Chinnor again. Anybody keeping the score? Must be about six trips, I think."

Still there is nobody to be seen at the station, except for Charlie, leaning on the door frame of the café. Melanie has an idea, which she puts to Maureen:

"Do you think we'd be allowed off the train to try and get into the gift shop? I think there are toys in there, something to keep the children occupied. It would reduce everybody's stress levels if they were happy."

The demon driver came in on the tail end of her suggestion.

"Happy? Is somebody not happy? I think it's been a particularly enjoyable day, apart from having to listen to this young gentleman."

He pulls Gary onto the train. Gary's mouth is firmly zipped shut, but his eyes are speaking volumes: angry, embarrassed, terrified.

"What have you done to my Gary?"

Gary's eyes go even wider at Ginny's outburst.

"Well, well, well. The embers of love are glowing again. But I must ask; did he learn English as a second language? I've never heard such a barrage of profanities. Almost all of his adjectives and adverbs begin with the letter 'F'. I can't be doing with it. Sit down, Mr Fotherby!"

Gary stumbles to his seat, with Ginny immediately fussing over him.

"You're not gonna leave him like this are you?"

"Oh alright! I suppose it will pose a problem if you two are going to, 'kiss and make up', I believe the expression is. But Gary; do not abuse the privilege of speech on my train," and then he turns wistful; "Aren't zips wonderful though? The gentleman that gave us the modern zip fastener, that was round about the time of your First World War; he buckled down to perfecting the design, pardon the pun, after his wife unfortunately died. Funny what grief can do, isn't it? I'm very excited to see if anything particularly good will come out of our forthcoming bereavement, aren't you? Keep those votes coming in, folks!"

Gary and Ginny's eldest child has started crying. Melanie steps forward to change the subject.

"Excuse me. Can I have a quiet word.? We were wondering if we could send somebody over to the station shop to find something to keep the children amused. I know they have toys and books in there."

"I suppose I have to listen to my Head of Customer Services. Very well. Whom should we send, do you think? Can we trust anybody to leave the train?"

"Of course we can. I know it's impossible to get away from you, or even to think about it without you knowing."

"True. As long as they know that….whom do you suggest?"

"A couple of the mothers: Ginny and Chelsea. They'll know what keeps their kids occupied."

"Good idea. And we have their children as hostages. I'll leave you to organise that, if you can manage to prise Miss Tucker away from Mr Fotherby."

"I'll go and find Chelsea and work my way back." As she moves down the carriage to do this, she is approached by Bella, who speaks in a whisper.

"Never mind toys. We need stuff from a chemist. My Keeley has just told me that she's, well you know, started her...um."

"Ah. I see what you mean. Leave it with me. I don't suppose he's factored that in."

After explaining the fun and games sortie to Chelsea and Ginny, emphasising the inadvisability of any escape attempt, she asks Ginny how long her supply of nappies and other infant accoutrements will hold out.

"Reckon I've got enough to last till the morning, if she doesn't get a dicky tummy again. Last night was terrible, so I put a few extra in for today. Always prepared, me."

"Great! You weren't planning to be here all night though."

"We seriously gonna be here all night? I thought it was just some big joke; y'know, like a reality TV stunt."

Good idea! If I can get this dumb bunny to think she's on telly, we might get through this a bit easier.

"Maybe you're right, Ginny! Some of the special effects are pretty amazing. I don't know how they do that thing with the zip. I'll have to ask. Now off you go. Take what you need and we'll settle the bill later."

"Oh cheers! And I'm sorry I called you a stuck-up cow."

"Not a problem." *I'm sorry I think you're a dumb bunny. Then again….*

She finds the driver drinking tea in Charlie's café. He gestures towards the seat opposite. She sits down.

"Excuse me….look…what do I call you? You don't like Mr E. You think Derek's all wrong. It's not really you."

"Sir, perhaps? A bit of respect?"

"Respect….okay., Sir. I have a request from one of the ladies. They need certain hygiene products and the children will run out of nappies, or do you call them diapers where you come from?"

"We've never needed them where I come from." He thinks for a moment. Then his purple eyes light up with amusement.

"I have a great idea. Can they hold on till morning, do you think?"

"Probably. What's the plan?"

"Never mind that. Find out if that van driver still has his keys. Maureen can ask him if you don't want to."

"You're not sending him out in a van, are you?"

"Dearie me, no. But I want his van. Off you pop." And he dismisses her with a wave of his tea cup.

"Right away. Sir!"

"And Jimbo needs to organise dinner."

Melanie turns back to say,

"They've been snacking and drinking all afternoon. What with that and all the stress, I'm not sure anybody has an appetite, but I'll ask."

When she returns to the carriage, Ginny and Chelsea have returned with books, puzzles, model cars, squeaky toys, cuddly locomotives; enough to distract their children for a while. As Melanie anticipated, even though it's now early evening, nobody is really bothered about dinner. A couple of the passengers put in orders for sausage sandwiches, which Big Charlie, in his track-side café, takes care of.

Jimbo is planning ahead. Taking advantage of the extra space in Charlie's kitchen, he's preparing a couple of one-pot meals that can be divided up and reheated tomorrow. The first problem will be getting the unwilling passengers through to tomorrow. The demon told them that wouldn't be a problem.

PART TWO

They Think It's All Over

Like many people with property to sell, I had always viewed solicitors and estate agents as a necessary evil. It's easy to have that view when somebody who is charging you two percent of your property's enormous value doesn't actually appear to do any work for you, work that somebody on minimum wage would do straight away if you asked them nicely. These days, even though my wife and I are embroiled in the tediously slow sale of our business, I'm prepared to give said solicitors and estate agents a bit of slack. Because I have experienced real evil. I don't know if it was necessary evil, but it was definitely evil.

My name is Chris Adwell. My wife, Trisha, and I have spent the last four years trying to put behind us the most bizarre and stressful experience imaginable. Sometimes, I wonder if I dreamt the whole affair, but, no; this happened to both of us. Funny; it started with somebody or something messing with my dreams. Turned out to be a vengeance demon that somebody had, what's the word? Unleashed? I didn't even know vengeance demons existed. So yes, unleashed in my direction, to punish me for some indiscretion on my part some twenty seven years earlier. I'd moved on with my life, for God's sake, happily married, good business, and then I find myself taken back in time, or taken into a construct of my past life, (I'm still confused about that), to face the music. Trisha was dragged into it too. From living the dream to living the nightmare!

Strangest thing though, and I know that Trisha doesn't really share my viewpoint, I actually found the demon feller to be rather good company, and, to give him further credit, he did eventually finish up protecting us from further harm. I don't know if vengeance demons have some sort of a guild and now he's been kicked out for going soft, but I'm grateful to him that my family remains safe and well. As I may have conveyed, my knowledge of vengeance demons is very limited. The only one I've encountered had developed an eye for a bargain, going to a café which offered deals on pots of tea for pensioners, and last time I spoke to him, by telephone, he claimed that I owed him a cup of coffee; which is true actually. I do.

The worst of the troubles that befell us weren't caused by him, but by the person he referred to as his 'client', who turned out to be somebody we had always thought of as a close friend.

Melanie Rainham had been waiting for years for the demon to punish me, and when it didn't turn out the way she wanted, she took it upon herself to burn down our shop and our house. And poison our cat. What had the cat done? When the demon stopped her, she was on her way to carry out an arson attack on my son's house in Birmingham.

Melanie hasn't been seen since. I'm not exactly sure what he did with her. It may have involved a chair, but I don't know for sure. We found it very hard to remain close to Melanie's husband, Greg, who was understandably mystified by his wife's disappearance, and very touchy about the police investigations into the arson attacks. And then he had his terrible cycling accident. We've kind of drifted apart. It's easier that way.

Our hardware store was eventually rebuilt and reopened, but in the aftermath of the fire, old Barbara, who had worked in the shop for years before we took it over, decided to retire. The young lad we had working for us part time, he had been thinking of having a gap year between finishing his A levels and university, but with his income stream being so rudely interrupted, instead of looking for another job, he had a rethink and postponed the gap year. His parents were pleased. I think he'd been spending too much of his wages on socialising anyway. But he was a bright lad, was James. I always knew he would go far.

Meanwhile, the solicitors and estate agents, taking full advantage of the bit of slack I'd extended to them, were slowly putting the finishing touches on the sale of our business and our cottage. We didn't have any cast-iron ties to the town we lived and worked in, and we'd always wanted to retire to somewhere near the sea, preferably one of the coastlines south or west of the country, based on the not necessarily scientific idea that the north and east ones would be colder. I'm not a scientist. I just like the west coast of Wales.

We were due to move out in about three weeks, but we thought it might be a treat to visit some of the places we'd never got around to while we were busy running our hardware store. Waddesdon Manor was impressive, a weekend watching classic cars racing at Silverstone was a great adrenaline rush. I've always wished I'd had a go at that when I was younger.

"So what's left on our list?" I asked Trisha. Well, her list really. She was a much better researcher and planner than me.

"Let's see," she puts her glasses on and runs a finger down her well thumbed and annotated A4 print-out. "I've got the Hellfire Caves at West Wycombe, but…"

"But no. Not for me, anyway. Something about the word 'Hellfire' brings back nasty memories of you-know-who. Besides, we've got a week of sunshine forecast. What's the point of spending any of it in a hole in the ground?"

"Fair point. That leaves a river cruise on the Thames at Henley. That sunny enough for you?"

"Cracking suggestion. Must take something for the ducks. Today? Tomorrow?"

"I'll see what's available." And she disappears into the dining room to look it up on the computer, returning about five minutes later with a furrowed brow and a disapproving pout.

"You'll get stuck like that if the wind changes."

"Very possibly," she says, but clearly puzzled by something that prevents her from enjoying my top quality joke. "I started booking a couple of tickets on a boat, and finished up booking tickets for a steam train ride instead. That's not even on my list. I don't understand it."

"Weird. Never mind. I rather like steam trains. The ducks will be disappointed though. Where is it?"

"The Chinnor and Princes Risborough Railway."

"Okay. Heard of that. Well, we've never been. Could be fun. When?"

"Tomorrow. Is that Monday? It's great being retired. I no longer have any idea which day of the week it is."

A Chapter of Revelations

Melanie was quite adamant:

"There's no way you're putting me to sleep again, not even for one night. Not after last time. I'll sleep when I'm good and ready, thank you very much."

"Just as you wish, but I wasn't talking about my staff, just the passengers. They'll be easier to control if they're unconscious, wouldn't you agree?"

Consequently Melanie and Jimbo found themselves, at the stroke of nine, the only conscious people on the train. The two demons had uncoupled the locomotive and taken it somewhere to stock up on fuel and water.

Jimbo comes out of the kitchen and supply area, carrying a bottle of Rioja and a glass.

"It's been a tough day. I was just going to find somewhere to take the edge of it, but you're welcome to join me if you don't mind melancholy company."

"Oh, why not?" She fetches another glass and follows him down the train to a private compartment that isn't already occupied by sleepers.

"Well this is nice," says Jimbo, pouring their first glass. "The man from the future and the woman from the past. Cheers!"

"Huh! That's by no means guaranteed."

"I thought you were on a promise, in a manner of speaking."

"In a manner of speaking. But I'd feel better if I had some details. I think he gets a kick out of dangling little bits of information. It's infuriating."

"Very. Meanwhile, kick off your shoes and get some of this down you. We're off duty for a while. Take the edge off. No idea what's going to happen in the future, but I'm just glad I'm here drinking this wine. Not sure I'll be great company though."

"Please! Don't apologise. Most of the time I can't decide whether you're a complete charmer or a total sleaze. The quiet side makes a pleasant change."

"Ha! That's funny, because I was a very shy and serious young man until after uni-grad."

"Is that the shy and serious young man you're hoping you can get away and find? He's probably still at the University, learning to be you. Perhaps I should find him first and warn him about the missing body parts. Anyway, what do you mean, you don't know what's going to happen in the future? You've just come from there."

He doesn't answer, just stares at something or nothing that's outside the window, then takes another gulp of wine without looking at Melanie.

"Why so serious now?"

"You probably wouldn't believe me if I told you. It'd sound crazy."

"Look Jim....Hang on! Can I call you James? I'm not part of your future television audience. Hope to God I never will be. Okay? Good….. So I've been held prisoner in a chair for four years and now we're on a train with a demon in charge and he's threatening to drive it up and down till Kingdom Come. That's what I call crazy. I very much doubt if you can top that."

"Wanna bet?"

In their short acquaintance (was it only a day or so?) she had found it hard to see James as anything much more than a bit of a clown; chauvinistic, abrasive, not her cup of tea at all really. Then she thought, guiltily, her husband could be a bit like that. Poor Greg. He was a bit of a showman too, but a lovely guy once you got to know him. James hadn't dropped the serious face.

"Try me then."

James looked at the nearly empty bottle. "We need another one of these. Back soon."

Melanie's body had lowered its usual tolerance of alcohol considerably; hardly touching a drop in four years will do that. She already felt like she was going fuzzy round the edges, but when James poured her another glass, she didn't refuse.

"So spill it…..I mean your….I mean, not the wine…..sorry!" She was trying to suppress a giggle, not wanting James to think she didn't take him seriously.

137

Something was obviously not right with him.

"You're trying not to laugh, aren't you? How long has it been since you had to do that?"

"I'm sorry. It's the wine. I'm not used to wine. Or laughing."

"No worry. I don't blame you at all. Anyway....you wanted to know my secret. Brace yourself."

"That bad?"

"Okay. I've told you a bit about the world going all 'World War Three: bring it on' and all the crazy shit in society, right?"

"Right."

"The thing is, I think it's all my fault."

There's silence for about five seconds, and then, "Is that it?" She's torn between laughing again, and some expression of disappointment. "That must be the biggest guilt trip of all time. And you were right; it does sound crazy. That's ridiculous. I'm sorry, but how could you be responsible for all that."

He's still not smiling, she notices. He shakes his head, the seriousness of his mood contradicted by the sparkling as his eye patch catches the light.

"Forget it. Let's just get drunk and hope things will look better in the morning."

"No, please. I just wasn't expecting that. I'll listen, I promise. You sound like you need to get it off your chest, whatever it is." *Play the sympathetic confidante card.* She puts her hand on top of his, and then moves it to the one that he was born with.

"That's my drinking hand. Thank you. So back in my first year at Oxford, (I went there to study history and political science), I met this North Korean student. Kim, he called himself. We were there for the same subjects and we got on pretty well. He was a bit odd, but then, to be fair, so was I. This would be about three years ago on your timeline. It was unusual for North Koreans to be educated abroad, but not unheard of. Kim Jong-un spent four years in Switzerland and France. He's their head man now, I recall. But my friend Kim wasn't too high profile. He was a cousin of the current leader and not in line to inherit anything. I think that he thought he was on some kind of top level spying mission, but he wasn't really all that bright academically. So anyway, one sunny weekend in the autumn, before our studies had really got going, we hired a punt from that place near Magdalen Bridge."

"I know it." She remembered how miserable she was when she walked past it a couple of days ago.

"Thought you would. So Kim, clowning around, the Mighty Kim, falls in and gets trapped under the boat, and me, the big hero, I jump in and save him. He'd have most likely died if I hadn't."

"Well done. So how is that a problem? I don't get it."

"You will. Scoot forward to 2035. The entire North Korean ruling family is killed by an assassin, a suicide bomber. My friend Kim is the only available heir. The bomber had connections with South Korea, so the first thing Kim does, hell-bent on revenge, is declare war on them, his army moving so devastatingly fast that the whole country is overwhelmed. The West would like to retaliate, but suddenly Russia and China are standing on the sidelines, smiling indulgently. At that point, whoever was responsible for dusting the Doomsday Clock needed to be pretty damn sensitive, we were that close to midnight. If the East rattled a sabre, the West had to rattle a bigger sabre, and that's how it's been ever since. And war's so good for business. The deep, dark money movers had no interest in discouraging it. Saving the environment doesn't pay nearly as well."

"Oh but seriously! Saving one person from drowning leads to the whole world being at each other's throats? Come on!"

"Well it happened in 1914, didn't it? The shot that sparked off The Great War."

"And you think it's all your fault. Wow!"

"No, Melanie. It's not his fault. It's yours."

Neither of them had heard the demon open the door and neither of them really took in what he'd just said at first. But James was the first to react.

"How can it possibly be her fault? She wasn't there!"

"Well tell her Jimbo. Tell her why you were at Oxford."

"I got the grades I needed to go to Oxford."

"But weren't you originally planning to take a year out?"

"True, but I had a change of plans after I lost my job….."

"You've just got it, haven't you? Well done. Shall I tell her?"

James can only nod. His face has turned remarkably pale for somebody with his swarthy Mediterranean complexion.

"Tell me what?"

"Jimbo lost his job because somebody burned down the hardware store where he worked."

"Oh my god!" Melanie's face has turned remarkably pale for somebody with her white-blond complexion. Nobody speaks. James is staring at Melanie, his expression hard to read. He eventually picks up his glass and leaves the room, muttering something about needing time to process this.

"James!" But he's gone before she can stop him. She looks at the demon, standing there with an infuriating half smile and raised eyebrows. "What's that look for? It's not funny. What am I supposed to say to him now?"

"Oh he'll be alright."

"Alright?! How can anybody be alright with you around? You set all this up, didn't you? You didn't just rescue him. You knew exactly what the link was between us."

"Of course I do."

"Of course you do, Mr Smug and All-powerful. I don't know what your plan is and I don't suppose you'd dream of telling me, but look; if you're so bloody good at controlling everything and everybody, why don't you just get rid of that Kim maniac?"

"I could. But where's the fun in that? Too easy."

"What? So it's all just a game to you. As long as you're having fun, to hell with the rest of us."

"No. May I remind you, we're not going there."

"Oh to hell with you and your nitpicking. I'm going to find James, Jimbo;…... whatever you wanna call him."

She eventually finds him sitting on a bench on the station platform, the wine glass, with its dregs, still in his hand. There is a chill in the evening air, and she anticipates an even frostier reception from James. But he apologises first.

"I'm sorry for leaving so abruptly. It was a bit of a shock. I just needed think-room."

Melanie is tumbling erratically into the conversation with her own apologies, until James stops her.

"We were right earlier. It does sound ridiculous. This whole butterfly wing-flappage, cause and effect rap; how far back are we going to take it? To the day I was born? He'd have drowned if James Reese hadn't been born? It's silly."

"When you put it like that….but look, I'm really sorry for what I did."

"Are you? You must have thought you had a good reason to burn down somebody's shop and house. And poison their cat too I understand. Sort of thing that anybody might've done. Wanna see my hit list for example?"

"Oh don't say that. It makes me sound like a terrible person. The worst."

"Are you though? A bad person, I mean. What would you say about me, the cannibal chef from the future? Am I a bad man? I mean I always thought that Chris Adwell was a good bloke. But you saw fit to wreak havoc on his life, so maybe he wasn't. And all these people on the train; they've done some pretty despicable things. Should we give them a score? Come on down! You've earned this week's star prize: Trapped on the Train. And you're through to Round Two: Murder Victim."

Melanie is only half listening, slumped on the bench, her head in her hands.

"I pretended to be Trisha's best friend for ten years. She trusted me…."

"Yeah. That is pretty bad."

They're silent for a while, and then James says,
"But he's told you it will all work out okay, yes?"

"That's what he said. But he's cruel. This is all a game to him. He likes to have his fun. And we just have to put up with it. We have about as much power as the pieces on a Monopoly board! I hate being completely powerless. Oh look! Goody! Here he comes again."

The door of the carriage had opened and the demon stepped onto the platform, the faint glow from his purple eyes very noticeable as he approached in the dark.

"So how are you both? As interesting as your reminiscences must be, I can't have my staff up all night talking. We have a train to run in the morning."

"You really are a heartless bastard, aren't you!"

"Am I, Mrs Rainham? I shall overlook that insult this time, in view of your stressful evening. But remember, I'm what you called a vengeance demon. What was it Sherlock Holmes used to say to Watson? 'You know my methods'? Well, you don't know mine. But you will. Just be patient. Now go and get some sleep. It'll put the roses back in your cheeks."

Gerald's Journal

Before I get started, I need to say I never done anything like this before, like keeping a diary. Weren't much good at righting at school. Good with me hands mainly. Fixin shelfs up for me mam by the time I were twelve. So one of them weirdo's thats running this shit show, the femail one, says I shud do this. Make it intresting, she says, something to keep your readers awake. Bugger that I thought but then, thing is, I dont mind admitting I'm scared. Scared for me life. Theres talk about bumping one of us off an I dont think there kidding. Maybe I shud right something down like evidents for the old bill.

And another thing. I dont need no stuck up toffee nosed Oxford bigwig telling me how I shud spell and whatnot, specially one that looks like a bloody pyrate and talks with a fake axent. Ive herd him talking normal to that Melanie. She's all rite btw. Bit of a looker. Maybe I shudna put that in in case the missus gets old of it. So whatever these are all me own words.

The missus, Bella and me havent been getting on very well of late. We been together about seven years and its not like I got the seven year itch that you hear about. Weed be great if it wasnt for that kid of hers, her Keeley. I mean I been around and happy to look after her since she was ate but now shes fifteen and knose it all like you do at that age. Course I'm not her dad and thats not good enough for her. Shes' off playing video games with that flytippers kid.

But this train thing is scaring the shit outa me and I dont know how to proteck me family and that includes her daughter from these sychos. I thought the first night was gonna be really crap. Most people didnt feel like dinner. I got a sausage sandwich to keep me strength up. That driver says how he's got a job for me and that prick Gary. I dunno what happened last night. It started getting dark. Some of the bairns were crying, poor little buggers. Next thing I guess we all went to sleep. Wouldnt put it passed them to gas us all. But everybody is up and lookin okay this morning. I can smell bacon and stuff. Its like a weird kinda holiday. Typical British holiday weather though. Raining. And now his nibs says he needs me and white van man for this job he was on about last night. I'll have to get back to this later I spose.

***

I'm back. What a fucking day scuse my French. I hate that bloody train driving old freek but I have to say he knows how to push all your buttons. So this was the job. After breakfast, full english with everything on it if their paying. That was my nickname at school btw Full English. Always a clean plate at lunchtime and clean anybody elsies if they had leftovers. So the train sets of again going to Princess Ris. Getting well board with that I can tell you. When we gets there he takes me and that Gary down the platform. Says he has a shopping list for us and theres a bloody great tandum that he expex us to go on. You cannot be serious I said. I mean that cargo bike was bad enough. And its pouring with rain into the bargain. The prick Gary chips in with how hes not riding that thing

146

looking at my fat arse. Normally i woulda chinned him for that but I dont think that would be a good idea today somehow.

So the job is for us two to take this boneshaker to the shops and get whatevers on the list which for Godssake turns out to be ladys sanitary products and nappies. The driver has to make it worse by telling me the ladys wotnots are for Keeley. Oh great I says. Shes gonna be even more moody if she finds out Ive been bying her tampons. Mega embarrassing I says. So we works out a deal. I tell Gary that he can have the front seat but he hasta do the ordering at the chemist. The only ray of sunshine is he looks even more miserable than me.

I bloody hate bikes and this tandem specially. It ways a ton and its not easy to ride with somebody you dont know. Probly not easy if he was your best mate which this guy aint. Its alright for them lycra clad twats with their carbon getups whizzing in and out of the traffic like they own the roads. But this thing was torture. We had to have a bit of a dummy run in the station carpark. I was tempted to put my feet on the handlebars and let the little runt do all the work but weed be so slow weed fall over most likely, so I did me bit.

Then just as we were getting to the end of the carpark this bloody white van swings in off the main road and nelly has us off. Bastard. That was my van Gary says. Never mind that I said, weev just got this thing going in a strate line with a bit of speed. So we kept going and managed to do alright until we got out onto Station Road. There's a nasty little climb leading up to a left hander and that bitch of a bike slowed right down on the hill. We were sweating cobs going up there but we made it to the top wobbling all over the shop. A bloke in a BMW gives us a blast on his horn, impatient bastard. You wanna try this mate I shouted, swanning about in yer flash car. Its not easy. He gave us the finger as he roared passed. Twat!

The rest of Station Road has always got cars parked down one side. Makes the road a bit narrer and then this white van pulls out and overtakes the lot on our side of the road. Him up front shouts, It's my fucking van again and look whose driving it. Its that woman with the purple eyes. Well he didnt say woman but I feel uncumftable writing what he called her. He wasnt happy is what I'm trying to say and I was nun too chuffed either. She nearly had us off. But the rest of the drivers were nearly as bad. We took our lives in our hands trying to get onto the main road. Cars squeezing between us and bollards, and a bus crawling up my arse. Very stressful. We was glad to get down the High Street and pull up outside the farmacy.

Gary was as white as the proverbial. You alright pal I asks? You look shell shocked. How do people do that evry day he says. Some of those bastards hardly gave us any room at all. Not easy having to swerve round all these bleedin puddles that cud have anythink in the bottom of em was how he put it. You know why we got this job, doncha? He nods and does one o' them smiles without being happy if you know what I mean. The next bit could be worse he says, holding up the shopping list. He goes into the chemist while I offer to guard the bike. Well we wooden want it to get nicked!!

He comes out two minutes later very red in the face. Smug looking cow in here wants to know. Light flow, medium, super. I dunno what he's on about. The tampons he says, like hes choking on the word. How should I know? Well shes your bloody daughter. No she isnt, and even if she was I cant ever see me having that kind of conversation with her.

148

Turns out he's got the list folded in half and all the gen is writ on the bottom of the page. Plonker. Still, rather him than me poor sod. Then I realised we probably coulda got all this stuff at Marks and Sparks or the Coop but I didn't have the hart to tell him that. The journey back to the station woulda been easier if it werent for me being loaded with carrier bags. We was starting to get the hang of the riding. Going down the hill weed struggled up was quite a blast. Okay. I admit I quite enjoyed it and we didn't see that van once. Like I said, normal traffic was bad enough. Can't think why we didnt even think about escaping or going to the police. Never entered me head. I asked Gary and he said the same. Not that he was a great one for running to the police at the best of times he says.

So there was the train waiting for us. We dumped the bicycle-built-for-two-complete-mugs hoping weed never see the damn thing again, handed over all the stuff weed brought and let them two weirdos know that theyd made there bloody point.

We gets back to the Chinnor end and finds some more people waiting to get on. Whats all that about?

That's Entertainment?

It's a shame, but charity shops frequently find it necessary to display a sign asking donors not to leave bags of items for sale outside the door when the shop is closed. Maureen was aware of this, which was why she was fully prepared to break into the charity shop on Princes Risborough High Street. Two or three in the morning was her preferred time to go shopping. Well, you avoid the crowds, for one thing. It was so nice picking the television for her flat, without some super-knowledgeable young sales assistant telling her that this model would be perfect for her and then trying to sell her an extended warranty for when it broke down.

CCTV on the street only revealed that somebody had entered the charity shop in the middle of the night and had loaded several bags from the shop into a white van. The somebody might have been a woman, but clearly one strong enough to open a locked door without using any tools or leaving any marks. When the shop staff arrived to open up, they discovered that every scrap of clothing had been stolen, leaving them with nothing but books, bric-a-brac and some old James Last and Vic Damone records, which were no more likely to sell that day than they had been in the previous months. On the plus side, there appeared to be a few Thomas the Tank Engine books which hadn't been there the day before.

Nobody had enjoyed a particularly comfortable night on the train; not the humans anyway. The train's bench seats are upholstered, but not to the level of a memory-foam mattress. A couple of the younger children were keeping people awake with their crying, but the advantage of a train is that, if you're quick on your feet, you can walk far enough away down the connected carriages to almost not hear the noise. Ginny said that her youngest would go off to sleep quite easily in a moving vehicle, and Maureen was able to kindly help out with that, as she had to pop out in Gary's van for a while.

Melanie had somehow managed to snatch short bursts of sleep, curled up awkwardly on the bench seat in one of the private compartments, but she was disturbed by her mind choosing to replay the conversations which she'd had the night before.

"I feel like I haven't slept for a thousand years," she told Maureen the next morning.

"Poor you. I know exactly what that's like."

James had been dozing on the platform bench, until the returning van had woken him up. It was either that or the rain, which had started to fall around four. Maureen hurried over from the van and thrust a tightly wrapped package into his arms. It was Ginny Tucker's baby, fast asleep.

"Make yourself useful, Jimbo. That's not a late night snack; go and take it back to its mother."

***

It's bad enough being held prisoner on an old steam powered train when your captor is a supernatural being

151

with apparently limitless powers and a twisted sense of humour. To make matters worse, there's no phone signal, no wi-fi, nobody calls in, nobody calls out. All the jigsaw puzzles are pictures of trains. A thousand pieces of monotony.

And today, it's raining. Just steady, soaking drizzle, no wind to drive it away, and the station is shrouded in mist. Even for people whose appreciation for the beauty of the Chiltern escarpment has become jaded by too frequent and too many viewings, the fact that they can hardly see anything through the dripping wet windows is disappointing. It would be hard to find anybody who could say they were looking forward to another trip up the line, even once. The first complaint of the morning came from Gerald, but not about the weather or the prospect of another stint shovelling coal.

"My mouth feels like I've been chewing a dead badger all night. And I didn't bring me toothbrush, needless to say."

"Good of you to say it anyway, Mr English." The demon just appeared at his side and handed him a brand new toothbrush, a tube of toothpaste and a bar of soap. "You can trot over to the little boys' room on the platform, and when you've freshened yourself up a bit, or in your case, a lot, you can be toothbrush monitor. We've got plenty."

Annabel Barnes complained that she couldn't possibly face the day in the clothes she wore all day yesterday and then, horror of horrors, slept in.

"Now don't worry about that, Mrs Barnes. Maureen has very kindly been out shopping this morning and has procured garments for everybody."

"There's just one thing," Maureen adds. "The shop I went to doesn't stock underwear of any description. So you'll just have to rinse your smalls in the sink." She points to the black sacks sitting in the corner of the carriage. "They're divided up into men's, ladies' and kiddies', but help yourselves. If you want to be non-gender specific, that's fine by me."

And so this strange prison rattled along; clothes and basic hygiene requirements thoughtfully provided, a choice of excellent breakfasts to start the day, all balanced with a total loss of freedom with no prospects of any change. Although one of their number was due to be murdered, they'd been told. That would make a change. So far, still only one vote had been cast. Melanie's antipathy towards Gary was still strong, but she was beginning to wonder if she had been a bit hasty. Her conversation with James the previous evening about who is good and who is bad had the issue of crime and suitable punishments occupying much of her thinking time.

And this whole situation she has found herself in. *It's just not worth it,* she thought. If she had never met this demon in 1991, had just kept her anger in check, accepted that her cousin's death was a tragic accident, she wouldn't be here now; a trolley dolly on a ghost train. Okay, Head of Customer Services, with a very smart uniform that seemed to refresh itself in the morning. She would still have to rinse her smalls in the bathroom hand basin like everyone else though.

She had been instructed to arrange the bathroom visits in such a way that only part of a family group was allowed to go there at one time; the other part remaining on the train in a kind of hostage status. She knew there was no chance of anybody escaping, but the demon figured that this way they wouldn't even think about it. Melanie wasn't entirely sure if that would deter Gary Fotherby. His sense of responsibility towards his family was clearly pretty shaky already, but the way he and his girlfriend had been steaming up the windows in their private compartment last night suggested that a bond might be redeveloping.. The ghastly thought occurred to her that, if the demon really did mean ad infinitum, they might be needing to turn one of the carriages into a maternity ward.

Her mind was going round in circles, coming back to the thought that she had recently voted to have somebody murdered, somebody who, however flaky, was the father of three, and potentially more, young children. Another hideous thought; if there was a murder victim, the whole point of a murder mystery party was figuring out who the murderer was. She wondered which one of them would get that rôle. This was like living in a nightmare. There must be some way to get out of it before she finished up being, at the very least, an accessory to murder. Her defence lawyer would have a major headache trying to explain the mitigating circumstances.

It kind of helped to have some common ground with James, although the common ground was her being an arsonist and him being collateral damage, so she needed to tread carefully with any conversations based on that. He seemed pretty chilled on the subject, but even if they did talk, that too involved going round in circles, unless he knew how to escape the demonic clutches. She wondered if the demon had a weak spot, like an Achilles' Heel, his very own Green Kryptonite. Perhaps something would happen if she said 'Derek' three times and stamped her feet. *That's the sort of thing my Greg would have said.* Greg was like that. Always trying to be funny when what was needed was something practical. No help at all, but she really missed him and hated having to wait for the demon to decide when it was time to 'put things right'.

Among the many things she didn't understand, the demon had said to her, it must have been when they were having breakfast in Charlie's café in Oxford, he'd said that she might have to reconsider her friendship with Chris at some point in the future. What the hell was that supposed to mean? Clearly the best person to talk to about her future was the demon, and that probably meant many more days of travelling up and down this godforsaken track. It was only day two and the novelty had already worn off, but not apparently for their mischievous host. Today's entertainment had been provided when Gerald and Gary had returned from their shopping expedition, dripping wet and very irritable and she'd even allowed herself a wry smile at their discomfort. She supposed they were being taught some tailor-made lesson rather than merely providing some impromptu Laurel and Hardy-esque spectacle.

Within half an hour, the train was back at Chinnor, pulling in with even more steam than usual as the rain evaporated from various hot metal parts. But instead of the anticipated quick turn around into another dreary journey, the timetable was interrupted by the distraction of a man and woman who appeared to be in a heated discussion with Big Charlie from the café. Charlie habitually took demonstrative shrugging way beyond French standards, so they gave up on him and turned to the arriving train. *I thought nobody else could see us.*

"Where are my children?" were the first words out of the woman's mouth, addressed to the driver, as he stepped down onto the platform.

The elderly driver seemed unfazed by the urgency of the question, instead advancing casually towards them with a warm smile; at least warm if his cold, purple eyes could be overlooked.

155

"You'll be Mr and Mrs Barnes, I expect, yes?" which took the couple by surprise. "The rest of your family is currently safe and well, and I'm sure they will all be glad to have your support."

"What do you mean 'support'? What's wrong with them? They should have all been home yesterday. What's going on?"

"Well Mr Barnes, or can I call you Philip? I decided that they would benefit from an extended sojourn with us."

"You….? Who the hell are you to decide to keep our children overnight? And we had no communication about any of this. I think I'm going to call the police. Have you got my phone, Dinah?"

"I doubt very much if you have any signal, even for emergency calls. It might be the weather. Why don't you come and talk to your charming Tony and Annabel? I'm sure they'll be able to tell you about what's been going on."

"He's right, Phil; there's no signal. Let's go and see the kids, like he says."

They were encouraged by the sight of Melanie, standing in the open doorway of the nearest carriage, smiling like the genial hostess that she had been appointed to be. Thus the number of people on the passenger list grew by two, who were escorted to the private compartments where the Barneses had fashioned a couple of bedrooms.

Five minutes later, Philip Barnes was out of the train and demanding angrily to know what the bloody hell was going on here.

"Are you completely insane? My dad has just told me that everybody here is being punished. For what? What gives you the right to kidnap people? And what are the children being punished for?"

The demon holds up a finger, which turns into a wooden spoon. Barnes is shocked into silence.

"My turn to speak." The spoon vanishes. "So many questions, Philip. I understand that. You're a concerned parent. Firstly, no; I'm not completely insane, although, to be technically accurate, no competent authority has ever taken measurements. Have you had it done? As to what gives me the right; well I have been asked by some of your fellow humans to mete out retributions that they weren't capable of, er…meting out. I freely admit that the exact methods are my own idea. And finally, the children. I just think it's nice for families to be together, especially in times of stress. Does that clear things up for you?"

Philip Barnes finds himself holding the wooden spoon, which he flings to the ground. The demon watches it fall and looks irritated, but catches it nevertheless.

"Is this about that fucking horse? It is, isn't it! Well there's a court case lined up about that. Isn't that punishment enough, for fucks sake?"

"Hmm. I've heard of a stalking horse, and a rocking horse, but not the kind you mentioned. Are all in your family so callous?"

"What the fuck are you on about?"

"There you go again. I find your language highly offensive."

"Oh do you? Well, up yours, Grandpa…."

Philip Barnes is treated to the same zip fastener experience that had worked so effectively on Melanie and on Gary Fotherby.

"Now that's better. Turn around, get back on the train and go and bring comfort and joy to your family. I have a train to drive. We will talk later, when you've had time to think of some more acceptable adjectives and verbs."

He heads towards his locomotive, but then turns to shout to Melanie, who is in the process of leading the terrified Philip Barnes back to the train.

"Send Mr Clark to me. I feel in need of a serious shoveller today. And then you and Mr DiRisso look after the passengers. Do your job! I'm going to check my cylinder cocks!"

Presumably they passed whatever checks that cylinder cocks require, and the train shortly headed back along the line, as it was to do repeatedly through the damp, drizzly day. But dissent was never far away. Tony Barnes and son collared Melanie as she was doing her rounds. Only a day or so into this what she could only describe as an alternate reality, and she had 'rounds'; checking on the welfare of the passengers *(huh! prisoners!)*, taking orders for drinks, clearing tables, picking up litter, washing up *(must get some of the prisoners on domestic detail before they start thinking it's a hotel)*.

Tony was really very agitated;

"Can you tell whoever's in charge of this shit show that I need to get back to my business. There are a lot of valuable animals that will need my attention."

Melanie was about to answer him and then she remembered why he was here in the first place and instead directed him to Maureen. The lady demon seemed to be all concerned as Tony explained his problem.

"There's just this girl that usually only comes in on Saturdays and she's not qualified to take care of all the animals by herself. My son was planning to be back there by the afternoon, but now….."

"What animals do you have there?" Maureen asked "I mean, I know you have chickens and horses. Or did have."

"It's mostly a petting farm, although there are a few Highland Cattle. But we've got pigs, goats, sheep, tortoises, rabbits, guinea pigs."

"And an alpaca, dear. It's just had a baby."

"Oh yes. Thank you Annabel."

"It's very cute, the baby."

"Yes dear, but I'm trying…."

"The children have decided to call it Pikachu."

"Annabel…..never mind its bloody name."

"There's no need to talk to me like that."

Maureen is enjoying this, looking from one to the other as if she's watching a knockabout vaudeville act.

"And there's no need….oh, look, I'm sorry, dear. There's no need to cry…"

"What are you talking about? There's every need to cry. We're stuck on this beastly train, while that poor little alpaca…."

Tony senses a small consignment of brownie points coming his way, if he's quick.

"My wife makes an excellent point. Some of our animals require specialist care, and I really don't know what will happen to them if we're not there to give it."

"So now we come to the nub, Mr Barnes, don't we? From my recollection, there's no guarantee that your animals would receive the care they need even if you were there. Or is it different for the cute ones, the money-spinners? But not the old nags. I hope he takes better care of you, Annabel dear. He might put you out to grass and find something cuter, eh!"

Philip, furious, intervenes:

"Who the hell do you think you are with all your insults and insinuations? You can't talk to my parents like that."

"I don't wish to debate that last point with you, but it is so refreshing to see a young man sticking up for his parents, right or wrong. But isn't it an interesting philosophy, loyally supporting somebody you care about, regardless of what they do?"

"What's your point about that? Is it a problem or something?"

"Not at all. Just that I've seen the same thing so many times in criminal gangs, nationalists, football hooligans."

"Are you trying to be funny?"

"Not at all. Do you think I'm funny? But I am curious to know if you support your father's neglect of his recently deceased horse. Y'know; family loyalty 'n' all that. But I think it's upset some of the other passengers, so maybe, now you're here, you should have a couple of these ballot papers."

"What ballot papers?"

"Haven't you told him about the vote, Tony? Well there's something for you to do with your afternoon. And don't go worrying about your precious animals. I'm sure they'll cope for a day without you."

"Ah good! So we're going home soon. It's about bloody time."

"Excellent! If that thought gets you through the day I'm not going to argue with you. Now Melanie here will take care of whatever you need to make yourselves comfortable, won't you dear?"

As she passes Melanie, clutching Gary's van keys in her hand, she whispers, "I'm just popping out to feed the tropical fish again. And I might look in on the new alpaca while I'm out. And see if there are any chickens I've missed."

"But why do you need the van? I mean can't you just…you know…?"

"Yes, but I've discovered I really like driving. Derek's got his train, I've got the van. Toodle-oo. Be good. Keep your hands off Gerald."

OMG

By the time Maureen arrives back at Chinnor to meet the train it is well into the afternoon. As she steps aboard, brushing feathers from her raincoat, Melanie and Jimbo are clearing away the debris from lunch, still with no help from any of the passengers. The general air of dissatisfaction, which was understandable, unfortunately also extended to criticism of the lunch menu. Jimbo had made a lasagne and had also discovered, behind the ticket office, a huge freezer, packed with 'quality' ready-meals. So the menu was augmented by cold poached salmon in a soy, ginger and honey marinade or an asparagus and feta tart, portions of which he'd been defrosting overnight in the fridge.

"I can't give my young'uns soy, ginger and honey marmalade."

"Marinade, Ms Tucker."

"Whatever. They won't eat it. Have you not got any fish fingers, that sort of thing?"

Big Charlie came to the rescue with that sort of thing, sausages, chicken nuggets and chips being his experience-based idea of what kids will eat. Jimbo wasn't too precious about his menu's cautious reception:

"To be fair, prison food still has the word prison in it."

Maureen, on her travels, had been back to her flat and found an old battery powered TV/VHS player, she said, in the back of a cupboard.

"How can you have that in the back of a cupboard, Maureen? You've only just moved in." The demon Derek, thought he knew everything, but this baffled him.

"Never you mind where I found it. I brought it along to entertain the kiddies."

Ginny Tucker steps forward to see what tapes Maureen has brought with her.

"It's years since we had one of these old tape players. What have you got for the kids?..... Thomas the Tank Engine.! Is there anything that isn't…..hang on. It says read by Christopher Lee. I thought Ringo Starr did Thomas."

"Try this one," a smiling Maureen hands her another tape.

"Ivor the Engine. Trains again! And that's bloody ancient."

"Yes, but this is the episode where Idris the dragon falls ill and Smaug from Lord of the Rings takes his place in the choir. Very dramatic ending. I recommend it."

"Is that it?"

"So far." Maureen seems a little put out by what she perceives as ingratitude. "In my experience, children will watch the same thing over and over again."

"But these sound like horror stories! What are the tapes in your other hand?"

"Oh they're for the grown-ups, in case we decide to have a film night. There's 'The Cassandra Crossing', 'Silver Streak' and 'Murder on the Orient Express'."

"I haven't heard of most of those. Don't tell me they're…"

"….all about trains. Yes."

The train stops again at Princes Risborough, and the driver comes back in with Darryl, who looks exhausted, after several hours of keeping the engine fuelled. Not being equipped with demonic energy, he needs a break, as much from being bombarded with information about Johnson bars and reversers and George Westinghouse's brilliant braking system, as the physical activity.

"I'm so glad to see you're all being looked after. Food. films and fun and games. And talking of which, I'm a little disappointed at the weight of the ballot box; still only the one nomination. Mr Fotherby is looking very nervous, I must say."

Darryl Clark whispers to Gary as he goes past, "If I have to listen to much more about the wonders of compressed air, I'll be voting for myself."

"I heard that, Mr Clark. Do you not enjoy our little chats up on the footplate?"

"Look pal, I don't want to be here at all. None of us do. If your idea of driving us up and down the line till we're all stark raving mad floats your boat, then good luck to yer. But don't expect us to enjoy it. We just want to get off."

"Funny you should say that, because I've been thinking about our Murder Mystery Night…."

"Not that again!"

"Yes, that again. The thing about these games is, not so much, who is the corpse, but who is the murderer. Obviously, one of you will have to do it, but…."

"What!" A roof-raising amount of noise ensues, like a release of compressed air, as everybody expresses their disbelief and disgust at once. Jimbo is standing next to Melanie in the doorway into their kitchen area.

"I can't see this lot developing Stockholm Syndrome any time soon, can you?"

"No, and sometimes I feel like I'd like to murder the lot of them myself."

"Hmm. Might make the Murder Mystery Night a bit of a pushover. Lacking tension and intrigue."

"But there'd be plenty of left-over food and drink. There's always a bright side."

The demon raises his arms in the air and achieves instant silence. Lips are moving, but no sounds come out.

"That's better. You really are an excitable lot. Now listen. I've devised a little incentive scheme for you. It might make…. Yes….what is it, Philip?"

"Are you completely crazy?"

"I think you asked me that earlier. Were you not happy with my answer?"

"I'm not happy, full stop! My father explained your insane idea. You can't seriously expect us to start killing each other."

"Of course not. Not en masse anyway. I just need one victim and one murderer. Is that too much to ask?"

"I was right. You are insane."

"He's very rude, your son. Should I blame the parents?"

Tony realises he's being spoken to, but, unsurprisingly, he supports his son: "We're not doing it and that's final!"

The demon shakes his head and shrugs.

"Frankly, I'm disappointed. You haven't even heard about my incentive scheme yet."

"Oh for fucks sake. Let's hear it then. It can't be any worse than all the shite we've already had to put up with."

"Why thank you, Gary. Very succinctly expressed, as usual. So here it is. Whoever volunteers to be the murderer, they and their whole family will be allowed to leave at the station of their choice, after the deed is done of course."

"I don't understand how we're going to choose."

"It's simple, Tony. Either Chinnor or Princes Risborough. There aren't any other stations."

166

"Not that! I mean, how do you expect us to pick a murderer and keep it a secret? I mean, isn't that how these things work? We've been on one before, haven't we Annabel?" His wife is too stressed to manage any more than a nod and a whimper, but if looks could kill, she'd be the murderer and the demon the victim. Finally she manages to speak.

"You've ruined our lives, you bastard. None of us want this."

"Really, Mrs Barnes? I would have thought this would be quite an educational trip for you all. Have you forgotten why you're all here in the first place, or do I have to go over it all again? Now, all stop talking at once and listen! This is how it's going to work."

Jimbo turns to Melanie and quietly observes, "He really likes that trick with the zips, doesn't he? I wonder what he did before they were invented. Buttons?"

"I'm glad you think it's amusing. I'm really not happy about this. It's bad enough being a trolley dolly, but now I'm having second thoughts about being party to a murder. I was pretty angry when I put my vote in, and I just wanted to make a point I think."

"Stop muttering, you two. Jimbo! This is where your interviewing talents will come in handy. Mr DiRisso here, will be taking up station in the last carriage and you will all take it in turns to go and visit him. If you wish to volunteer your services to, how shall I put it?, broker your family's freedom, then it will all be done discreetly; without giving the game away, as it were. Everybody understand that?"

"Why do we all have to go and see him? He gives me the creeps."

"Because, Mr English, if only the would-be killer went it would spoil the game a bit, wouldn't it? Bit of a giveaway."

Mustn't spoil the game; that would never do. Melanie decides she has to have some answers about where this is all going. The tedious punishment of trial by locomotive is sadistic enough, but this is going too far.

"I suggest you all get cracking. The game is scheduled for the night after tomorrow."

"Oh great! What day's that?"

"Monday of course."

Jimbo shrugs his shoulders, and turns to Melanie, looking as unhappy as she does about this new development.

"I suppose I'd better go and set up the confessional then. Sorry to leave you with the washing up."

"Don't worry about that; I'm going to press-gang some help. I'll bring you a pot of coffee if you like."

"Urr! Oi hopes it's as hot as you are. Sweet 'n' taystee is ow oi likes 'em."

"Don't do the voice, or I'll get Gerald to deliver it."

***

The afternoon returns to its regular monotony of enforced rail travel and noisy childcare. The demon sometimes referred to as Derek suggests to the demon Maureen that she could enhance her skills as a children's entertainer by reading them some Bible stories. He even lends her his own well thumbed copy.

"What a good idea! Infant Bible Classes. I can give them a bit of moral guidance while their parents are off volunteering to murder somebody."

The tedium is relieved a little bit by the trickle of interviewees gradually becoming a stream. Melanie wonders if they're all suddenly keen to play, or whether it's just something to do that beats looking out of the window. Surprisingly, she has a volunteer to help with the domestic chores. The surprise is that it's Ginny Tucker. It can be a difficult working environment when the person you're working with knows that you have voted for their partner to be murdered. The conversations won't be about the weather, or holidays.

But Ginny is fascinated by the whole scenario on the train, having convinced herself that this whole experience is the latest manifestation of the genius of reality TV.

"I just can't believe we got picked."

"Er, no; I was a bit surprised by that myself."

"Really? I thought you were part of the production team."

Oh my God! I'm going to have to tread warily here. "Oh yeah, I see what you mean. Yes, I'm crew. I meant I wasn't expecting to get the Head of Customer Services job."

"Well, you got the look alright. Hey, I'm glad it's not Love Island. I can't get into my bikini after three kids. Anyway I'm glad to get a break, even if it is doing the washing up. That Maureen's looking after the kids at the moment. She's a scream, that one. Do you think she's really getting on a bit, or have they just made her up like that?"

"Oh, she's definitely getting on a bit."

"Uh huh. So there must be hidden cameras everywhere. They're so good at it these days, aren't they? And the special effects! I thought my head would literally explode when we all got our mouths zipped up! It was almost like it was real. Amazing, their make-up department."

Good grief! "The best. And those glowing purple contact lenses he wears. What about them?"

"He's a character, eh? Must be fun to work with. You known him long?"

You could tell this woman anything. "Oh, about four years, on and off. He hasn't always been easy to get on with though."

"That's celebrities for you, I suppose. I'm looking forward to watching it all on catch-up when we get home. What's it called again?"

Bloody hellfire! Big Buffer? Thinking on her feet, Melanie comes out with, "Perpetual Locomotion." Ginny looks blank. *You don't do puns, do you?*

"I think that's the working title. It'll probably be 'Chained to the Train' or 'Chuffed to Bits' I can't remember…. Ginny! Are you enjoying this? I mean, going up and down the track, day in, day out."

"It's alright. Makes a change from what I usually do. I mean I get up, microwave the kids' breakfast, walk to pre-school, drop the biggest one off in year one, walk to a playgroup or some mother and toddler thing, walk back to pre-school, try and remember to eat lunch, walk back to school at three, faff around on the swings and what-not, beans on toast or something, then try and get them off to sleep."

"So it's just like this, but with better food."

"Oh, The food! You're telling me! I can't afford stuff like you've got here. It's a real treat."

This strange, less than secure, bonding experience was interrupted by the sounds of some childish distress from further down the train.

"That sounds like my oldest. Sorry; I'll have to go."

***

Ginny meets her five year old running towards the kitchen area, in tears. His crying is setting the other two off.

"What is it, precious?"

"That lady's gonna chop us in half."

"What!? What have you been telling my kids? Look at the state of them. I thought you were supposed to be telling them Bible stories, for goodness sake."

"I was," says Maureen. "It was the story about King

Solomon, where the two mothers both claimed the baby was theirs. So he suggested cutting it in half, so they could both have a bit. Very practical, I thought."

"That's horrible! Couldn't you read something that won't scare them? Goldilocks! That sort of thing."

"Bears! There's a thing in the Bible with bears in it!" She flicks through the ageing copy until she finds the reference.

"Here it is, in the Second Book of Kings, chapter two. A bunch of kids were insulting the prophet Elisha, so he called down evil upon them and two bears came out of the woods and tore forty-two of them to bits……. I see what you mean."

"That's even worse than…"

"But they could do with learning some manners to be honest. It's very educational, don't you think?"

"Never you mind my kids' manners! What happened to all the Thomas books? Come on, baby," she says, snatching the little one from Maureen's lap. "We'll go and play somewhere else, and then I'm going to see that pirate bloke."

"I think you just lost a fan there," says Melanie to a slightly bemused Maureen. "She thinks we're on a reality TV show and you're one of the stars, would you believe?"

The train chugs the last few hundred yards towards Chinnor once again, and Jimbo walks through from his interview room, seeking coffee and a chance to stretch his leg.

"I've just had that Ginny Tucker woman in, asking if I can add any names to the voting slip. What have you been saying to her, Maureen?"

As the train slides in alongside the platform, Jimbo looks out of a window and notices a couple standing near the ticket office door.

"More people? Oh my God!"

Melanie looks out to see what has provoked his outburst.

"Oh my God!"

With Friends Like These…..

I was looking forward to our day out on the train, with a school-boyish enthusiasm, which was a relief to Trisha, who had felt a bit guilty about booking the wrong tickets. We assembled a flask of coffee and a couple of peanut butter and banana sandwiches, anticipating that there was unlikely to be any vegan food available. We're not particularly hardcore about the vegan thing. It's funny how vegans always seem to be described with an adjective from the porn industry or from the world of laying concrete driveways. Anyway, we like to be prepared in case the only option is a bacon sandwich. I'll admit, I like the smell, but I always try to see it from the pig's point of view.

As the forecast had said, the morning was bright and warm, and so we loaded ourselves into our venerable Audi and headed towards Chinnor. The car had done us proud for well over a decade now, but we kept debating whether it was time to get on the electric vehicle bandwagon. I found myself wondering if bandwagons would have to be electric from 2030 as well. I mentioned this to Trisha and, predictably, she just pulled a face and didn't laugh. But if I catch her passing that joke off as her own……

"Maybe we should wait to see what the charging network is like where we move to. We don't want to be stranded in the middle of nowhere."

"I thought that was exactly why we were moving. Peace and quiet at last."

"You know what I mean!"

"Of course, a lot of people think that electric cars are the wrong way to go; bad for the environment. All the precious metals that have to be mined or something. They say we should be driving on hydrogen power and then we'd only get water out of the exhaust pipe."

"Hydrogen. That's not laughing gas, is it?"

"No. I think that's nitrous oxide."

"We should use that. We'd get more smiles per gallon."

I shook my head in disbelief.

"What?"

"That's the sort of thing I would say, and you'd pull a face and tell me it was a rubbish joke. Obviously, the way you tell it makes it much funnier."

"No. You're right. It is a rubbish joke……but I'm just googling 'hydrogen' and the first thing I see is that it's highly explosive. I don't fancy driving round, sitting on a bomb."

"You mean, as opposed to petrol, which is dead safe. Look what it did to our property. I don't know. I was a cook and a hardware store owner, not a rocket scientist. I guess we have to trust somebody to do something to save the planet from disaster. I'm just glad it's not my job. I mean, I like to do my bit….."

"Though it would look good on our gravestones when we finally go, wouldn't it? **'Chris and Trish: We'll miss them. They saved the world'.**

"Not if it means being buried with my underpants on the outside of my trousers. Talking of fuel, I'll just pull in here and fill up."

The Chinnor filling station was only about a mile from our destination, but I took advantage of the lack of queue at the pumps and put a few gallons in. Trish went in to pay for the fuel, and as I sat in the car looking into the shop, I thought that the old boy serving behind the counter looked somehow familiar, although with his extensive grey whiskers and dark glasses, and the reflection on the window, it was hard to place him.

Trisha got back in, looking slightly puzzled.

"What's up, flower?"

"The old feller said, 'Good to see you again'.

Again? We've never been here before. "But he'd turned to the next person in the queue and I got sort of shuffled out of the shop. Oh well. He probably says that all the time, or his eyesight's dodgy and he mixed me up with somebody else."

But I felt the first spiders of something I couldn't put my finger on crawling up and down my spine. I don't really like putting my finger on spiders anyway, but I wanted to see if I was just imagining things.

"Hang on a sec." I pulled the car away from the pumps and into a parking space. "I'm just going to pop back in and see for myself."

When I entered the shop, the old man was nowhere to be seen. I asked the woman whose badge told me she was a Team Leader and who presumably had replaced him, if he was still around.

"Old Derek? He's gone on his break. Should I let him know somebody's asking after him?"

"No, it's alright. We just thought we knew him from somewhere."

"Well here, probably. He's worked here longer than I have, and I've been here six years."

"Sorry. My mistake."

All the way round the corner and up the hill to the railway I hoped it was indeed a mistake, but when we parked the car and waited on the empty platform, I knew that it wasn't. I don't know why what should have been a platform bustling with day trippers was completely deserted, except that the timetable on the wall informed us the next train was on the following Sunday, not today. Or it could have been that the train driver, who smiled and waved as he brought the train to a halt, and was definitely somebody I recognised, had arranged it that way. He was good at arranging things. I was right about the spiders.

Trisha felt my tension.

"Chris! You look like you've had a shock. What's wrong?"

"I have had a shock, and I really don't know how to prepare you for one either. So, brace yourself."

"What are you talking about?"

I didn't reply, because the engine driver was walking towards us from the signal box end of the platform. I hadn't seen him in this task-appropriate clothing before, but I recognised the wrinkly face and slight smirk. And the purple eyes. He approached with his right hand extended, as if to greet an old friend. A little presumptuous, I thought.

"Mr Adwell! Or may I still call you Chris?"

"I'd rather you didn't call me at all! I was sure I'd seen the last of you. Hoped…..What the hell are you doing here?"

Trisha is looking from one to the other, presumably waiting to be introduced, or perhaps not:

"Chris! This is the old man from the petrol station…."

"Yes, but without the false beard and dark glasses. Am I right? What was all that about?"

"I just wanted to get you in the mood, so to speak, before we met."

"Oh you did that alright. But it's not a very good mood."

Trisha is pointing at him with a shaking hand and I'm hoping he'll excuse how bad mannered that is.

"Is this who I think it is?"

"I know what you're thinking, and yes, I am."

Trisha pauses for all of three seconds before slapping him hard with her right hand. Jesus! I wonder if any living soul has ever done that to him before, but she probably only managed it because he let her. Out of sympathy?

"You fucking arsehole!" Wow! She might be pushing her luck a bit now. There's not much I can do except wait and see. I don't think it'll come to me pleading for her life to be spared. He clearly has some purpose in bringing us here. I'm not sure if I'm that keen to find out what it is.

"I think I can let that pass this time," he says, rubbing his cheek; "The violence and the language. Dearie me."

He turns and gestures towards the door of the station's snack bar.

"I completely understand that you may have questions and possibly hard feelings….."

"Too bloody right I've got hard feelings….."

"Mrs Adwell, or may I call you…...?……no, perhaps not….but come and sit in here for a while. There's somebody I'd like you to meet, but I need to, how shall I put it? …set the scene first."

He turns back to shout something towards a young man who is leaning out of the cab, or whatever it's called. "Mr Fotherby! Do the cylinder cocks for me, the way I showed you." I realise how little I know about steam trains.

We allow ourselves to be led into the snack bar and seated at a table. "I'll see if Charlie can rustle up some drinks for us?"

"Charlie? Surely that's not….."?" About four years ago, this demon had taken me through some sort of alternative

179

version of my past, which still doesn't make complete sense to me; never mind. But he did take me to a coffee bar run by a guy called Charlie. I'm sitting with my back to the counter, so I swivel round, and there he is; the same man. This is getting surreal; well, it already was, so quite frankly, what did I expect?

"That's not who you wanted us to meet, surely?"

"Nice to see you again, Sir."

"Er, yes, you too, Charlie."

"A while since you were in my caff."

"Indeed." I'm not sure if it's four years or thirty-one. Like I already said, I haven't entirely figured out this alternative-past/time-travel scenario.

Trisha is still fuming, but I'm guessing that underneath all the anger she's as scared as I am. We both know what he can do if he feels like it. So she brazens it out.

"So what are we here for? This had better be good, or we'll….."

"You'll what, Mrs Adwell? Slap my other cheek? I don't think so. But you said it had better be good. I think it is. I want you to help me save the world."

It's funny, isn't it? There I am, full of apprehension about whatever mind-messing situation we were about to find ourselves in, courtesy of this very disturbing character. But I needn't have worried. He just wants us to help him save the world. I look across at Trisha; she's looking at her right hand, either wondering if she could get away with doing it again, or wondering how she got away with doing it in the first place.

"Well don't both talk at once. I think that's an amazing offer, and neither of you have anything to say. Well really!"

I elect myself spokesperson.

"Sorry….yes. It's funny. We were only just talking about saving the world on the way here. Little did we think….. What the heck are you talking about?"

Trisha finally stops palm gazing and joins in.

"That's ridiculous!" Well that makes a change; she usually says that to me. "You seem to go out of your way to hurt people, not help them. Now you're saying you want to save the world. I don't get it."

"Obviously not. Permit me to explain something about us demons. I know the popular image. People think of us as evil beings, eternal torment, pitchforks and hellfire, blah, blah, blah. All the clichés. But that's not the case. We just happen to have special skill sets which humans who wish to inflict evil upon their fellows find it useful to employ. It's the humans that contact us that are the evil ones, if you ask me. These days, they seem to think we're available at the mere click of their fingers. We're just filling a niche market; it gives us something to do. Stops us getting bored. Er…human hands making work for idle devils, if you get my drift."

"I wish I'd thought of that line," although I realised that, out of context, it wasn't much of a joke.

"Ah, Chris. D'you know, it's people like you…..what I mean is, I quite like the human race, by and large, and I wouldn't want to see it wipe itself out, and not just because

I'd have to find something else to wile away the centuries. Human activities are very entertaining."

"Aren't we just? I remember you having great amusement at my expense. Never do something the easy way if you could have fun watching me floundering about in the mire. Anyway....why do you think the human race is going to wipe itself out?"

"I know it is. I've been there. You've got thirty years before human society ceases to function in any meaningful way. I suppose I could work with the few survivors, but it seems a shame to lose so many good people, don't you think?"

"What do you mean, ceases to function?"

"Just that. What was that expression we used to hear about your weapons' capabilities? Mutually Assured Destruction. But there's somebody I want you to meet who can explain why that's going to happen."

"Who is it?"

"In a minute. Aren't you interested to know what I want you to do?"

"Okay. What do you want us to do? I'm not wearing my pants outside my trousers."

The demon is clearly irritated: "This is serious! Kindly channel what's left of your short attention span. I could do it myself. Save the world, I mean. But as a courtesy, I've decided to bring you in as consultants."

We look at each other; Trisha and I, that is. I'm so glad I've retired and I don't have to submit my CV to anybody these days. He sees our confusion. A blind person could see our confusion.

"I need your advice."

For a moment there I thought he'd said he needed our advice, but even allowing a few seconds for the part of my brain that understands things to catch up with my hearing, the confusion doesn't go away.

"You're confused."

At last, we're on common ground.

"Yes, we're confused," I said, assuming I could speak for my wife too. "In our admittedly limited acquaintance, you gave me the impression that you knew everything, and have the power to do everything that you want to do. Don't tell me you have a weak spot."

"Weak spot!? I just told you, I seem to recall, that I can save the world without you. I'm asking for your input as a courtesy, a friendly gesture, if you like."

Trisha's definition of the word 'friendly' is clearly at odds with his:

"Friendly? You don't know the meaning of the word!" I'm sure he does, but I'm not going to interrupt. "What you put my husband and I through was definitely not friendly."

"Surely it wasn't all bad, Mrs Adwell. A unique bonding experience, I would have thought. And I did save your husband's family from a hideous fate.

"Okay. I'll grant you that. And you did get that devious cow Melanie out of our lives for once and for all."

"Ah…."

"And you're right about one thing; it's the people that employ you, if employ is the word I'm looking for, that are evil. I'll never forgive her for setting fire to our cottage. And killing my poor cat!"

"Ah…. Look, before we go any further, there's somebody I'd like you to meet. Would you be so good as to wait here while I fetch him? Another flat white, Mrs Adwell."

It's not a question; it's a statement. Trish looks down at her cup, which has another coffee in it. I've seen this trick before, but it's still impressive. From behind the counter comes Charlie's "Oy!".

"Sorry Charlie. I'll settle up later." Charlie rolls his eyes. "He gets upset when I give coffee away. Back in a minute."

I still didn't have a clue what was going on, but I'm used to that. The demon's responses to Trisha's minor rant were quite strange. I thought for a moment he was going to produce Melanie Rainham, so I was extremely glad when he indicated that the person we were about to meet was a 'him'.

And the gentleman in question was ushered into the room, a stocky individual a good bit shorter than I am, looking quite nervous, and looking a little strange too, with a sparkly, black eye-patch. He came towards us, limping very slightly I noticed, his hand outstretched to meet mine.

"Hello Mr Adwell, Mrs Adwell. It's good to see you again."

Again? Not another one. Although there is something familiar about him.

"I'm sorry. I can't recall where we've met."

"I'm not surprised. I'm James. James Reese. I used to work for you in the hardware store."

"James? You can't be James. He's, what? twenty-one, by now, and you're….."

"Forty-nine. I know; it doesn't make any sense does it? But…"

Trisha interrupts, but her voice is full of tension.

"What was the name of the lady that used to work for us?"

"Barbara. She retired after the fire at the shop."

Trisha rounds on the demon.

"You could have told him that." The demon is slowly shaking his head.

"No, this is your James alright, although most people call him Jimbo. To cut a long story short, I brought him back from the year 2050."

Trisha sits down, I sag back onto the edge of our table. Not bloody time-travel again. Charlie hurries over to take the cups away, for safety's sake. I still don't understand why the demon needs our help, when he can organise

185

time-travel.

"Jimbo? James? What the hell happened to you?"

"It's a long story, as they say. I don't want to go into details, but our mutual friend here saved my life."

"Friend!?" Trisha is still struggling to accept a vengeance demon as a friend. "I don't understand why everybody thinks this…this…whatever he is, is our friend."

"Hang on a minute, Trish! I agree with you," (a good tactic, I've discovered), "we're probably not putting him on our Christmas card list. But, as barmy as it sounds, he said he wants our help saving the world. He probably means it. He's just brought James back from the future. He can probably save the world too." And then I had another thought: "James! Shouldn't you be at university in Oxford right now?"

"I almost certainly am. It freaks me out. I have no idea what would happen if I met myself, but all the sci-fi I've read said it was a bad idea. But I can't see Uni-me coming here for the day somehow. Trains weren't my thing."

"It was motorbikes, wasn't it?"

"Yes! It was. Hey!...Do you remember….?"

"Stop!" Trisha screams. "Never mind all that! What the hell are we all doing here? If Mr Super-power or whatever he is can do so much, why are we here at all? Get back to the point. Please!"

"It's Derek."

"What?"

"I'm not Mr Super-power. Some people call me Derek."

Trish finally finds something that amuses her in all this. "Derek the demon?" Now we're all stifling giggles. Except…... Derek.

"Don't try my patience. I've brought you here because I am about to change the course of history. My problem is, I can't decide at which point to change it, and it's going to affect all of you, very acutely. That's why you're here. Like I said, out of courtesy, you can help me decide which version of your timeline you like best."

"We were quite happy with our lives until about an hour ago, thank you very much. We've sold the house and we're just about to move to a little place in the middle of nowhere. Don't you go mucking it up. It's been bad enough dealing with buyers, vendors and estate agents."

"I understand all that, Mrs Adwell. But were you quite happy with the events of four years ago? Your property losses and so on?"

"Oh, you mean all the crap that you inflicted on us. Thanks again."

"May I once again point out that it wasn't me who lit those fires……."

"Please!" I try to get the meeting back on track. "Trish! and…er….Derek!…. Derek? Okay with that?"

"Not really, but you have our ear now."

"Good. Why the hell are we here? Why is James here? Are we supposed to have a debate on how you're going to 'change the course of history', as you put it?"

"It's a massive responsibility, isn't it? James; tell them where you fit into all this."

And so James, over the next ten minutes, explains his part in the boating accident that saved the life of the future Korean leader. I thought I could see where this was going, but I couldn't help thinking that there must be an easier solution, and I said so.

"I think I can see where this is going, but I can't help thinking there must be an easier solution."

"Of course there's an easier solution. You're going to say, why don't I just get rid of the Korean fellow. But where's the fun in that?"

"Where indeed? Well heaven or hell forbid that we should spoil your fun. What bloody ordeal have you got planned for us this time?"

"Oh there's no blood involved. But I do have to admit, Chris; I've managed to get us all into a situation that even I find mind-boggling."

I've never seen him looking baffled before. I rather like it. Or it's a bit worrying. Both….

"So what's the problem? You, me, Trisha and James have to decide how to change the course of history so that the future world despot drowns?" How do I make something so utterly crazy sound as easy as picking lottery numbers?

"The problem is, I made somebody a promise. It's me, you, your good lady wife, James….and one other. She's very much a part of this….."

"Mrs Adwell? Are you alright?"

Trisha has gone white and starts to shake. I put my hand on hers. "Trish. What is it?" And then, like some resting chameleon, my hand goes white too, when I realise what she's just seen.

Melanie Rainham is standing in the doorway. She looks pretty shaky too.

Looks Can't Kill. Try Poison

A familiar expression 'If looks could kill'; it's not entirely relevant here, as I could only see the back of Trisha's head, but her hair was standing up in a very expressive way. I remember reflecting once on the idea that hell hath, (although I usually say has), no fury like a woman scorned. I'm sure our demon host could contradict that. But I thought at the time, that it's not so much the arson or the pet poisoning or the murderous intent, so much as the fact that her supposed best friend has been deceiving her for ten years. Or maybe I'm wrong.

Trisha leapt out of her seat and covered half the distance to where Melanie was standing, suddenly cowering, in a flash.

"You bitch! You killed my cat!"

Melanie, not having any further she could reverse unless she went back outside, just said, "I'm really sorry."

She sounded very meek, very contrite, but I didn't think it was enough really. Clearly, neither did Trisha.

"You're sorry? Do you have any idea what we've been through? I mean, apart from the cat and the fires?"

Melanie looks pensive, as if something had just occurred to her.

"Actually, I don't. I never thought to ask…..him."

She indicates the demon, who has strategically moved to a spot between the enemy camps.

"No, she didn't ask me, which I must admit, I thought was strange."

"That's probably because she's a selfish cow who only thinks about what she wants. I'll tell you what happened shall I? Chris got taken back in time to meet his ex-wife, for some convoluted reason, and then I finished up tied to a chair in some dingy little room for a whole night."

At this, Melanie finally retaliates. "One night? Only one night? He had me there for four bloody years!"

"What!?"

"You heard! Four years! And then he wakes me up and tells me that Greg is in a wheelchair, and I can't go back and see him till some time, God knows when, that suits His Satanic Majesty here."

"I like that! It suits me better than Derek."

"Four years?"

"Yes, four miserable years. So, yes, I know I've put you both through hell, but there must be some kind of statute of limitations. Don't you think I've paid for what I did?"

Trisha doesn't have any immediate reply, but suddenly rushes towards Melanie, who jumps to her right to avoid what she assumes is an attack, but Trisha is heading for the door.

"Oh, don't worry. I'm not going to add to your misery. I can't handle this. I'm going to wait in the car."

James and I hadn't really said anything during all this. I looked at him and we did a bit of synchronised head-shaking. I was thinking that the demon, or His Satanic Majesty, as we were probably going to have to start calling him, was expecting us all to work together to save the world. I looked at Melanie, who was now sitting on a chair in the corner of the room. I didn't have any warm thoughts for her either, but she looked like a puppy that had had a good kicking. I wouldn't have minded betting that she wished she'd never started all this.

Actually she looked like a kicked puppy that had dressed up as an air stewardess. (Are we allowed to say '-ess' these days?) What's all that about? I decided to risk 'Derek' again.

"Derek." A cold stare. I can live with that. "What's with the uniform? And the train, come to think of it?"

"It's very simple. Melanie is my Head of Customer Services on the train. And isn't she lovely?"

"Melanie?"

"No, you fool; the train."

I take a look out of the window.

"It's not exactly the Flying Scotsman."

Another cold stare. Perhaps I'd better not push my luck.

"It's a beautiful little engine. Best I've seen in a while. What do you mean, customers?"

"Oh you must come and meet them. My passengers are a bunch of accursed examples of human degradation. I'm treating them to a free train ride, fully catered. And their wives and kids are here too of course."

"Of course!" What the heck are we getting into now? Pure speculation is suspended for a moment as Trisha re-enters the room. She still looks pissed off, if a bit less stroppy with it.

"I couldn't open the car."

"Is that your doing?"

Derek takes a bow. "Nobody's going anywhere until I say so. We need to work together. Even you two!" He indicates my very unhappy wife and the even more unhappy Melanie, who is now sitting weeping into a hanky. I'm finding it all a bit moving, but I've always been a soft touch for a damsel in distress. Then I remembered the cat. I'm not lending her my hanky.

"I can't work with her." Trisha is quite adamant, and the demon flashes his purple-eyed anger at her.

"Have it your way then. I'll make all the decisions by myself. But I'm giving you fair warning; don't blame me if your timelines get completely………buggered up!"

His hand flies to his mouth, his eyes are screwed tight shut, caught in mid gaffe. I don't think any of us dared say anything. It was far from being a bonding moment, but we shared the surprise. The demon opened his eyes, looking annoyed with himself now, as well as everyone else.

"Mrs Rainham," he practically barked. "Back to work, if you will. We have a railway to run. Mr DiRisso, you too. Mr Adwell; I'll leave you and your wife for an hour or so to decide what you want to do."

"We just want a quiet life."

"Do you, Chris? But where's the fun in that, eh? Live dangerously!" He smiles his humourless smile and then vanishes back to his train, leaving us looking at each other, feeling helpless. Live dangerously. Great! We're not on our own for long. A woman's head pokes through the door.

"I do hope I'm not intruding." The intruder, as the rest of her followed her head, was a woman in late middle age, I would say. A little bit younger than me, anyway. I'd describe her as sensibly dressed, a bit plain, but that's being unkind. We're not supposed to judge a book by the cover, are we? She's probably beautiful inside. And then I notice the purple eyes. Probably not beautiful inside.

"Don't mind me. I just came to see if Charlie had a tiny little bottle I could put some of this in," she says, indicating a large bottle which bears some sort of hazard warning label.

"How about one of these whisky miniatures?" Charlie produces a tiny bottle with a picture of a bell on it.

"Ideal! A great disguise. Would either of you fancy a splash of this in your coffee? The whisky, I mean. Not this. It would kill you quick as a flash. Ha ha ha!"

It's a bit early in the day for whisky, especially a blend, so we decline the offer, and the woman downs the drink in one quick swallow. As she carefully trickles a few drops from the larger bottle into the small one, she introduces herself as Maureen.

"Or Mo, to my friends. I hope we can be friends."

A demon called Maureen. Or Mo. Friends?

"What the hell is going on, er…Maureen? We've just been sitting here, talking about saving the world, and now you're planning to poison somebody. Is that right?"

"Oh yes! We're having a Murder Mystery Night on the train. Too bad you've turned up too late to vote, but the passengers have finally elected a victim and somebody has volunteered to be the murderer, so we're all set. It'll be fun."

"And that's real poison?"

"Of course."

I wished I'd taken her up on the offer of that small whisky now.

"Fun? There's a very strange idea of fun around here!" But again, quite frankly, what did I expect? From my own experience, I knew that the demon derived great entertainment from watching people under stress, even if it all worked out well in the end. Nobody leaves until he says so, he'd made plain. Stressful enough.

Trisha asks, "How long have the people on the train been here?"

"Just a few days, dear. Not long."

"Not long! Nobody books a nine mile train ride lasting a few days!"

"Oh we've only just started. They're certainly getting their money's worth, aren't they?"

Trisha and I just look at each other. The lady demon watches us with that irritating demonic smile, and then says,
"I know what you're thinking."

"Yeah. We know that."

"Stressing people out is one thing. Getting them to kill one another is a bit too far, yes?"

"Pretty much," I replied, as Charlie placed a couple of unopened miniatures beside our cups. Has he started reading my mind too?

"But it'll all work out well in the end."

"Great! How can killing somebody work out well in the end?"

But I'm starting to piece together bits of the conversations we've had since we arrived here: timelines, changing the course of history. Us being here as consultants is a bit hazy though.

"I think I've sussed it out, Trish. At least, some of it. He's going to use time-travel. Is that it, Maureen? Your victim gets murdered and then you wind back to the start of the game?"

"Well done, Mr Adwell! You're certainly on the right lines."

"So you could just play the game over and over again. Ad infinitum. I'm not sure how that's going to save the world."

"Well, he doesn't tell me everything." I bet he does. "The only way we're going to find out is to discuss it on the train. But I know this, Trisha dear; you are going to have to find a way to work with Melanie, whether it suits you or not. In fact, both of you, remember; most of the problems you've had were because she didn't think you'd suffered enough. So don't make the same mistake she did. Because that girl has suffered, believe me. Ooh, I'm getting all misty-eyed now. I'm losing touch with my demonic side, listening to you people and all your weird hang-ups."

And with that cautionary synopsis, she left the room, clutching her bottles and looking a tad flustered. From my previous experiences, I knew we would have no choice but to go along with whatever the demon, or now demons, for crying out loud, had planned for us. We were trapped. But to try to keep the mood congenial, (or is it convivial? I'll look it up if we ever get home) I had to ask,

"What do you think of our demons so far?" remembering that Trisha had never met either of them before.

"Oh they're great! An eighty year old train nut with a twisted sense of humour and some flaky woman who looks like she runs the local W.I. How could it be any better? I assume these are disguises."

"I suppose so. I've only met the one before and he's always looked like an old man. I'm not sure we want to see whatever they're hiding. But it doesn't really matter. The biggest issue now seems to be whether we can find some way to deal with Melanie. It looks like they're forcing us together."

"I'd like to deal with her alright, the scheming cow."

"Yes, I get that, and I'm not happy about her either. But I don't think he's joking about this 'saving the world' idea."

"He jokes about everything else. You've heard him. 'Where's the fun in that?' he says. Are you sure this isn't just another one of his lunatic wind-ups?"

"I don't think so. James seems convinced that it's the real deal, and him just being here tells us that these demons can move people through time. What bothers me is that I don't think we're talking about just doing reruns of a parlour game. I think he's going to start messing with our past."

"But that's going to change the present. We don't want that to happen, do we?"

"Well given that, at present, we're stranded in a railway station with no hope of escape, I'm not so sure. We have to find out what the plan is."

"Which means working with Melanie, yes? God! I could strangle her!"

"Ah, but we're going to save the world, aren't we? Superheroes don't have to like each other. Haven't you ever read any Marvel comics?"

"Never."

"No? You've never been tempted to leaf through my stash in the landing cupboard?.....No; probably not. I don't see you doing that somehow. But we have to find some common ground with Melanie, open some sort of dialogue, like it or not."

We can hear the sound of the train approaching the station, and, with a nod of thanks to Charlie, we reluctantly take ourselves outside to see it coming in. Whatever fate awaits us, I do like the sight of a steam locomotive arriving in a station.

Catching Up

The locomotive glided majestically alongside the Chinnor station platform, or as majestically as a little green 0-6-0 engine that is nothing like the Flying Scotsman's usual tractive power unit can. His Demonic Majesty, Derek, somehow conferred some of his status upon his current favourite toy. But in the train behind the engine there was no such regal atmosphere. Trouble had been brewing since the previous evening. That would be Monday evening.

The reason for the trouble, apart from the usual air of unhappiness that emanates from a group of prisoners in the early days of their incarceration, was a rapidly developing relationship between Keeley and young, but not little, Charlie. Having discovered a mutual interest in games that could be played on a tablet or phone, they had entered into a world of their own, a world in which adults were superfluous and was fascinating enough to render them largely untouched by their confinement on the train. But even this activity lost its attraction after dozens of hours played non-stop, and Charlie had reached that age when he had noticed that older teenage girls had, quite appropriately given the location, 'more curves than a scenic railway'.

The quotation may have been taken from a book by P.G.Wodehouse which neither of them would likely have read; the activity in which they were caught indulging would not have. As her mother's partner, Gerald, dragged her roughly out of the compartment in which he'd found her and Charlie, she protested.

"Let go of my arm, you fat bastard. We were only kissing."

Indeed, as she said, they were only kissing, but Gerald decided that it was unwise to allow a fifteen year old girl and this scheming twelve year old Lothario to develop their friendship any further. Probably not wrong, but his mistake, for his personal future well-being, was to humiliate Keeley in front of the other passengers, stopping, as he did, to call in on Darryl and Chelsea Clark to denounce their son as morally defective. The parents of the two miscreants may have remembered their own youthful days, when they engaged in similar activities in their burgeoning romantic careers, but the passing of time and the accumulation of what passes for wisdom seem to absolve some people of their sins and have them impose the rules which they'd spent their own teen years kicking against.

Thus Keeley and Charlie were grounded, with instructions to keep well away from each other, which they mostly complied with, except that Keeley managed to pass a note to her erstwhile boyfriend, urging him to find one of his parents' voting slips and fill it in according to her instructions. It is frequently heard from mature people that young people don't want to work, an expression of prejudice taken up by subsequent generations. But young Keeley found plenty to keep herself occupied after she and Charlie were forcefully separated. Busy, busy. After writing a note for Charlie, and filling in her mother's ballot paper, and a second one she found, discarded by another passenger, and depositing them in the box, she went to see Jimbo to volunteer her services as murderer, and then, pleasing her mother, who was extremely happy to see her daughter bouncing back so cooperatively after her rebuke, went off to take Ginny Tucker's place helping with the catering. Charlie wasn't too happy, of course, and he had no idea what was going on, but twelve year old boys don't usually.

***

The next morning, which would be a Monday, the occupants of the train noticed another couple of people standing on the platform, a man and a woman, sixtyish, probably husband and wife.

"Two more flaming mugs." moans Tony Barnes. "What we need is the S.A.S. not a couple more passengers. How come nobody, the police, anybody, has turned up to look for us? I don't get it."

He does observe, however, that the new people seem to know the driver, even if they don't look very pleased to see him. He couldn't argue with that point of view. The woman actually slapped his face. Tony winced, thinking that, after seeing what he'd seen, he certainly wouldn't recommend that.

The train was standing for longer than usual between turnarounds while first the driver and the new people, and then that weird chef bloke and then the stewardess woman took it in turns to disappear into the station café. When the woman came out, she was looking very upset about something, and then the train set off again without picking up the new people. How come they managed to avoid this accursed railway journey? Perhaps they were the same as the driver, had the same powers. You just couldn't really tell anymore.

But when the train arrived back at Chinnor about an hour later, the couple were still there, and this time, they were shown into one of the carriages towards the back of the train, away from most of the other passengers and into one of the private compartments. Derek calls everybody else together, telling them he has a number of announcements to make.

"Good morning, everybody. You will no doubt have noticed that we have two new guests this morning. Our family's growing!..... Unlike you, they're not here to be punished, but because I have a matter I need to discuss with them, which will very definitely affect some of you. But while they're here, they will be enjoying the same level of hospitality and quality catering that you have. Their names are Mr and Mrs Adwell; Chris and Trisha, and I'm sure you'll find them excellent company.

Moving on, we at last found ourselves a victim and a murderer for this evening's entertainment. I would have liked a few more votes to be honest, but there was a clear winner anyway. Or perhaps loser might be the right word. Dinner will be served at 7.30 sharp and the game will commence very soon after.

And the other big news is that some of you will be leaving us tomorrow, but I'll keep the identities to myself for now."

Once again, a general hubbub of questions raises the noise level beyond what is comfortable. As if he's leaving a press conference, Derek just throws "No more questions, ladies and gentlemen" over his shoulder, as he beckons to Melanie to follow him.

In the quiet of the corridor he turned to tell her,

"It seems that Mr Adwell is finally ready to talk to you. So that's good, isn't it?"

"If you say so. Not his wife?"

"No. She may need a little more time I fear. In here," he says, opening the door to an empty compartment. He leaves Melanie on her own while he goes to fetch Chris.

***

"Here he is. I'm sure you two have lots of catching up to do, and I've got a train to drive. Be good."

Chris enters the compartment, his demeanour very awkward and apprehensive. Melanie is sitting staring at the floor, feeling like she is about to be interviewed for a job she really doesn't want and that requires qualifications that she just doesn't have. She decides some eye contact might make the process go better. What she didn't expect Chris to say was,

"I'm really sorry about Greg." Melanie manages to rein in the sob which is threatening to bubble up and overwhelm her.

"Thank you." This is not the subject that she thought they'd be discussing. "Have you seen him? I mean, recently."

"No; not for a long time. Things got a little difficult after…..well, after you left. He wasn't very happy about you being suspected of arson, and even more unhappy about us going along with the police's suspicions, so….things got a bit tense. But it was terrible about his accident."

Melanie's battle to keep her composure is lost.

"Everything's gone wrong….. I've ruined everything. I don't blame you for hating me. I never thought that all this would happen, believe me. I'm so sorry!"

"Take a breath, for goodness sake. I don't hate you. I don't know what I feel right now. I can't speak for Trisha though. But I'll pass on your apology, for what it's worth."

"No need for that. She can tell me herself." Melanie and Chris look round, surprised to see Trisha standing in the doorway. "I hate getting second-hand news, so I thought I'd come and see what pathetic excuses look like for myself."

Chris sighs, more than a little disappointed to see his well thought out diplomatic opening being overridden by his wife's decidedly more gun-boat version.

"What happened to you, Mel?" Words of concern, but delivered with icy hostility.

"I…I told you…"

"I don't mean the chair thing. I mean, what happened to you that made you spend years pretending to be our friend, and then you put us through all this shit?"

"I don't know what to say. I was just so angry when my cousin died….."

"Yeah, yeah, yeah. And you blamed Chris. Chris bloody well blames Chris. But even if he'd actually killed her with his bare hands there's a legal limit to what you can do. It doesn't involve supernatural beings, setting fire to property and poisoning a cat."

"When you put it like that…."

"I do put it like that!"

The flow of conversation dries up, until Chris says, "And our demon host says we have to work together. To save the world, no less. Hmmm."

"And about this bloody demon we've had inflicted on us; life has got very complicated since he got involved. I know he's got almost godlike powers and I know you think he's good company over a cup of coffee, but really! He makes everything so….so, like I said…complicated."

Trisha pauses for breath, but neither of the other two feel like saying anything; Melanie because she doesn't feel her opinions will be given any credence just yet, and Chris, because he's never had to referee a conversation between his very angry wife and the woman who made her very angry and has only this morning come back into their lives from a four-year-long 'missing-presumed-dead' hiatus. He feels like he lacks the necessary experience. So Trisha continues.

"This train! What's that all about? Sounds like some sort of mobile prison. And you're Head of Customer Services? What in God's name is going on?" she asks Melanie, who is glad to be on more neutral ground.

"That's exactly what it is. He's got a bunch of people here that he's been given to punish and he's just driving the train up and down the line, day and night, and nobody can get off. It's his idea of fun, mixing business and pleasure. Apparently, he's always wanted to drive a train."

"Good grief! So where do you come into it?"

"He woke me up from the chair and told me that I could either stay there indefinitely, or I could be a trolley dolly."

"A trolley dolly?"

"His exact words. Head of Customer Services was just tarting it up a bit. It doesn't make me feel any better. Whether I'm stuck in that chair or stuck on this train, I can't do anything for Greg. He doesn't even know I'm alive."

And, as if the floodgates have opened, she tells them how her daughter had summoned the demon, how the two demons had joined forces to fill the train with passengers and how inventively cruel the pair of them were. She tells them about each of the passengers and why they are there.

"Worst of all, the fourth one, Gary Fotherby, is the person who knocked my Greg off his bike and put him in a wheelchair."

"What!?" Trisha is on the verge of saying, "You poor thing" but catches herself; she's not ready for overt sympathy yet. "I see what you mean about cruel."

"Chris!" says Trisha. "You're not saying much."

Chris has just been looking out of the window and giving the women space to communicate.

"No, I'm listening though, and really enjoying the scenery to tell you the truth. I can't believe we've waited so long to do this."

"You wouldn't be so keen if you'd been going up and down the damn thing for the best part of a week. Ad infinitum is what he told me."

"No. Sorry. I suppose not." He holds up his hand to try and forestall an interruption and, to his surprise, it works. "Look, Melanie. I don't know if we can ever just draw a line under all the stuff that's happened between us. Like Trish said, I've been beating myself up about Yvonne for years, but your reaction was completely over the top. But we need to shelve all that for now, because it seems we have to work together. As ridiculous as it sounds, we have to save the world."

"It does sound ridiculous. If it wasn't for James being here, with his news from the future, I'd be more sceptical."

"From the future. That's what I don't like about this 'saving the world' lark. I think somehow it's going to involve time travel. I bloody hate time travel."

Gerald's Journal

I'm quite getting into this writing thing. Dont spose I'm ever gonna be much good at it, not like that socalled pirate feller. But they do say its quite therapeutic. I bet nobody I know back in the reel world wouldav expected me to be able to spell therapeutic, but I asked for a dictionary from that Melanie, and she was very obliging. Funny innit how difficult the word dictionary is. I had to look it up. Is that irony or something. Reminds me of that song Hole in my bucket.

I'm still hoping that all this might be used as evidents against this pair of loonies what have got us all trapped on this boring bloody train pardon my french. Two more people turned up today. I hoped it might be from the old bill, but it looks like its a couple that everybody on the train crew seems to know. Wooden surprise me if they turned out to be demons too. That's what Tony said anyway. He's the bloke what let his horse die. I dont hold with croolty to animals but Ive chatted to the bloke once or twice and he seems normal enough. You never can tell I says. I always thought I was a normal sorta person but Im stuck here for just expressin me onest opinion. Shit appens.

And Im in more bad books at the moment after I found our Keeley and that flytippers brat snogging in the back somewhere. Nipped that right in the bud I can tell yer. They can look all the daggers they like. Its for there own good.

Talking of daggers there still talking about this murder misery thing thats supposed to be on tonight. They must be having us on. No way can they really kill any body. I voted for that Gary, just for a laugh reely, partly cos he poked fun at my big arse when we done that bike ride and partly cos Melanie did. She thinks I'm an influenza so……its not much of a reeson. But she certainly influenzas me.

Any road up, I done as I was told and went to see the great jurnalist. Obvious that its a smokescreen to hide the chosen killer, if there is such a thing. I said Id like to ring the train drivers neck and he sais hed put me on the waiting list. Smart Alex.

I mite have to come back to this later. Seems I have to take my turn in the loco today. Dont spose shuvelling coal is gonna do me back much good but its quite interesting trying to figure out what all the levers and dials are all about. That evil old feller seems to know it all anyway.

***

So im back. Not easy washing all the grime off in the station bogs. Only a couple of hours before the murder party gets going. I can right about what happens tomorrow. But theres a big row going on somewhere. I swear I just herd somebody say You cannot be serious. Swear to God. Like that bratty tennis player from back in the day. Mighta been that new guy that turned up today. I think his missus is in there and Melanie and the pirate. Every now and then you can here the driver stopping all the arguments. Big voice for a little bloke, but then he aint normal is he. I think the noise is coming from the caff on the platform. I could murder a bacon sarnie right now but Im saving meself for dinner. Think theyve got something special cooked up.

Negotiations

Trisha and I were introduced to the other passengers. A mixed reception, to be honest. I think one or two people looked as if they welcomed the break in their boredom. One young lad asked me if I'd come to rescue them from the monster. I rather lamely told him that I would try, but it was sad to see that this young kid's life had been possibly indelibly scarred by his encounter with this supernatural creature.

"But Mister! Have you ever seen him do the change thing? So cool."

Maybe not indelibly scarred then.

I realised that I actually never had seen that. I'll have to ask for a private showing.

It would perhaps have been more courteous on 'Derek's' part if he hadn't taken great delight in telling us what everybody was 'in for' when he did the introductions. Or maybe he could have levelled the playing field by referring to me as 'Chris; the man who let his mistress die because he put the phone down when she asked for help'. Something like that. Gary, whom I probably won't be permitted to call 'Gaz', shrugged us off with a contemptuous observation that if we weren't able to get them out of "this shit show" we weren't much use to anybody. It's nice to be appreciated.

One of the inmates kept staring at us, the one called Gerald, or 'the internet troll', to use the demon's helpful thumbnail description. Eventually I realised that we knew him too.

"You used to run that hardware store, didn't you? The one that burnt down."

"That's right." I noticed Melanie, busy in her customer servicing activities, tense up and turn her attention to our conversation.

"Did they ever get anybody for it?"

"Not as far as we know."

"Makes you wonder what we pay our council tax for. The police are bloody hopeless. So the firestarter got off scot-free?"

"Oh I don't know. Maybe their conscience keeps them awake at night." Melanie is avoiding making eye contact with anyone.

"Nah! That sort are the scum of the earth, ruining a small business like that."

"I remember you now….Gerald, is it? You used to come in quite a bit. Hardly ever bought anything. Said we were too expensive compared to the DIY hypermarkets."

He had the decency to look slightly embarrassed.

"Ah, if only we'd had the buying power of a

hypermarket. That's the problem with small businesses in small towns. And everybody loves them, but doesn't think how much it costs to make them work." I can get quite boring when I get one of my hobby horses out of the stable.

"Tell me about it." This interruption came from the man whose name I didn't catch, but I remembered that he was 'the horse killer'. "Tony Barnes", he said, holding out his hand. "I heard what you were saying about the cost of running your own business. The pandemic nearly crippled us, what with lockdown stopping anybody coming to our farm. The animal feed bills still racked up though."

Well this is nice. Cosy, almost. We're a distraction from the usual monotony of relentless rail travel, somebody to air grievances to, but all we need now is for the fly-tipper chappie to start blaming charges at the waste disposal sites for his own antisocial behaviour. We've all got an excuse, haven't we?

Trisha is looking uncomfortable, to some extent because she's still struggling with Melanie's presence, but also because she's trying to avoid being climbed on by a couple of dishevelled toddlers. It's funny how people who don't particularly go a bundle on small children or dogs will be targeted by both. But then she is approached by another, somewhat older little girl, who hands her a picture she has drawn and seems very proud of.

"It's him," she says. "The driver. What he looks like underneath."

Trisha shows me the picture. Maybe I won't ask for that private showing.

Lunch has been served, and cleared away by the train's crew, James, Melanie and a teenage girl by the name of Keeley, who seems very enthusiastic as a waitress. And when she's not busy, she's talking to the other demon, Maureen, who seems to have taken the girl under her wing. I must check that little girl's picture again.

I can see how the novelty of being reacquainted with our nation's transport heritage could soon wear off. We've only been up and down the line a few times today and I'm already tired of craning my neck to see into the backs of the Chinnor houses that line the track. So it comes as something of a relief when the demon parks the train at Chinnor for a while and calls us to order for a conference. By 'us' I mean Trisha and me, and Melanie and James. Maureen is left in charge of the passengers.

"As long as she keeps away from me and my kids with her bloody Bible," I hear one woman complain. Not sure what she means by that, but, not my problem. My problem is, my sinking feelings tell me, somehow tied up with time-travel. I had always been very sceptical about even the possibility of travelling through time, or to use a more modern and economical phrase, is it even a thing? Until I met the demon, 'Derek', His Satanic Majesty; now, anything's possible. Not necessarily desirable, but possible.

We enter the café once more. I'm on the verge of asking Charlie if he has a loyalty card scheme, but the demon goes to organise some coffees, and then James takes over that task because of an unpaid tab. Derek is in a bit of a bad mood as a result of that exchange when he comes back to the broadly spaced semi-circle we have arranged the chairs into.

"That's just great. All the trade I've brought his way over the years and he won't even extend my credit to the price of a pot of tea. He was just as stingy when he was running a Lyons Corner House between the wars. Those places were open twenty four hours a day and I knew a lot of individuals back then who didn't like to go out in daylight. I always took them there; but what thanks do I get? Now, Chris. I understand you have some concerns about this evening."

Of course he understands......

"Yes I do. Are you really going to kill somebody? It's not possible to just act it out?"

"No it isn't. I mean it could be acted out, but I can't wait to see the looks on their faces when they realise they have a real dead body on their hands. And I'm not doing the actual murder anyway. We have a human volunteer who was more than willing. But.......you know what I'm going to say, don't you Chris?"

"I think so. You're going to say that it won't matter because you're going to undo the death with good old time-travel."

"Well done, young man," he clasps his hands together in mock glee. "And I think you've probably all worked out that there's much more at stake than just a silly parlour game, as entertaining as that no doubt will be. I'm going to wind things back a little further than a few hours. As I see it, we need to prevent this Korean dictator from ever having the opportunity to get his hands on a position of authority. That's the main goal. And that should be enough to save the world. For now anyway. Yes, Jimbo?"

"So I'm right in thinking your plan is to engineer a situation where I don't finish up at Oxford at the same time as Kim, and therefore I don't save him from drowning?"

"Exactly. But there's more at stake than that, because I made a promise to Melanie here, and let's face it; if you don't keep your promises, what's your reputation worth, eh?"

Trisha and I looked at each other and shook our heads. In our book, he had a reputation for screwing up our lives, creating hideous nerve-wracking problems for us, and even if he did help us to find our way out of them, the stress has probably already taken years off our life-expectancy. So, reputation? Hmmm. But I knew we had no choice but to hear him out. I think he liked the sound of his own voice too much not to continue anyway.

"Chris and Trisha! Pay attention, because this idea of mine will affect you. Obviously the best way for my plan to work is for Melanie not to set fire to your shop, way back in 2018. What do you think of that idea?"

He said that as naturally and as glibly as if he'd been selling us a second hand car; 'tell you what, I'll chuck in four new tyres and a full tank of diesel. How does that suit you?' And it sounds like a great offer, but still the idea is scary. I don't know how to answer him.

"What's the problem with that? I thought you'd jump at the chance to have your life back. What have you got to lose?"

Our sanity, if this keeps up.

"So you're saying we'd get to keep our shop, our house...."

"My cat!"

"Of course, your cat."

"James would keep his job and put off going to Oxford for another year and….."

"I would never meet Kim."

"Therefore you couldn't save him. Thank you, James."

I still have a nagging feeling that there's something not right about all this, but Derek carries on.

"And Melanie benefits too. She doesn't disappear out of her life and consequently her Greg won't have his cycling accident and finish up in a wheelchair. Happy! Happy! Happy!"

We all look at Melanie, who by now should be radiating some of the Happy! Happy! Happy! that we've just been hearing about. Instead she's nervously chewing her bottom lip and looking at the floor. The demon takes up the reins of the conversation once more.

"Melanie, however, has proposed a different point in time to go back to, haven't you? Go on. Tell them."

Melanie is clearly nervous about this, but then seems to stiffen her resolve and, looking me straight in the eye, she says,

"The summer of 1991."

I wasn't expecting that, and it takes a moment to sink in, but when it does it sinks like Mentos in Coca-Cola. I almost overturn my chair as I leap to my feet.

"You cannot be serious!"

"I am. Dead serious."

"But that's…..that's.."

"It's just before you let my cousin Yvonne die. I want to go back and make sure she doesn't."

What am I supposed to say to that? "I don't want you to prevent your cousin dying"? I look at the demon, the chairman of what must be one of the most important meetings in world history, the Chinnor Summit, and I find him sitting there with that irritating smirk he has, obviously enjoying my discomfort. Did I say discomfort? Agony would be a more accurate word.

"Looks like you're finding this amusing, as usual."

"I'm finding it fascinating, I must say," says the demon, as if he's looking at tiny life forms through a microscope. But Melanie is growing in confidence with her sales pitch. I don't know if she expects to get anywhere with her suggestion, but she's on a roll now, directing all the sarcasm and hurtfulness she can muster at me.

"It could be the making of you, Chris. Maybe you and Yvonne would get back together and then, ooh, I've just thought; we'd still meet socially now and again, cos she was my favourite cousin. That would be nice. Or maybe you would patch things up with your first wife and go back and bring your little boy up properly. Obviously there wouldn't be much chance of you meeting her." She turns to glare at Trisha, who easily matches the hostility.

"You vicious bitch. You'd love that, wouldn't you?"

"Too right I would. And I'd be fine because I met Greg before it all happened. Anyway, what's the problem?

219

If he takes us back to 1991 you won't know anything about your life up to now. See what I mean?"

I can't believe how casually she spouts this twisted logic. Surely the demon, who says he quite likes people, isn't planning to go along with this. It's outrageous.

"Of course we won't know about it. But we know now! You're suggesting we allow you to take away the last thirty years of our lives. What? Am I supposed to look Trisha in the eye and say "here's a good idea, goodbye and I'll never see you again."? Worse than that; never mind again. The chances of me knowing her at all are almost non-existent. There's no way I'm agreeing to this."

"Do we get to vote on this?" James interrupts with this question. "Because I can't go along with Melanie's idea either. I understand her wanting to prevent her cousin dying, but the consequences are just too…….too far-reaching. And too cruel."

"Thank you, James. Exactly my point. The whole idea's preposterous." Then I decide to really push the boat out and turn on the demon. "In fact this whole thing is ridiculous." I've had people, my nearest and dearest included, tell me that something I've said is ridiculous, I think I'm owed a few. I'll risk His Satanic Majesty's disapproval.

"This train idea of yours. If that's your notion of how to get back at people, driving them up and down a very short railway track till they're all stark, staring bonkers, so be it. Who am I to judge? Probably more effective than suspended sentences and fines."

"Don't try my patience, Mr Adwell."

"Oh, dropped the 'Chris', have you? No more Mr Nice Demon? Well now you're trying our patience. Bringing us all together again to decide how much of our history we can afford to discard! Like James said; it's just cruel."

"Not just cruel. I'm very good at cruel. But it's funny, don't you think?."

"Funny!?" Both sides of the temporal clash joined in the chorus, but when the noise died down I knew we would still be singing from different hymn sheets. (If I ever get the chance to write a journal, I'll leave that hackneyed phrase out.)

"It's funny watching you humans dealing with the consequences of your misdeeds. And then I suggest a way to put things right and you don't want to do it. I completely understand why God has given up on the place, bless him. People doubt his existence because blah, blah, blah if there was a God he wouldn't allow all the suffering….okay, do things my way….oy! Don't interfere with our right to independence. So, yes. It makes me chuckle."

There we all are then, probably all struggling to see the funny side. It's true, isn't it? You can't force somebody to share your sense of humour. I couldn't count the number of times Trisha has failed to respond positively to my excellent puns and one-liners. But she does have a knack of cutting to the chase, as she proceeded to demonstrate now.

"Can I just ask? It's a question about this train, or really, about some of its passengers."

"Of course you can, Mrs Adwell." The demon hunches forwards, on the edge of his seat. "Go on."

"We were talking to some of your prisoners earlier. It just made me think. The van driver, Gary, and the one you called the internet troll. How did they get here?"

"I believe one of them came in a van and the other one on a bike."

"That's not what I meant, and you know it."

"Sorry. A little joke, if you will."

"Just trying to delay the inevitable, more like."

"Do you know, Chris? I think your wife's the bright one in the family, I really do. Good for you. Lucky man. Anyhow…..where were we? Ah yes. If I recall rightly….."

"Of course you do."

"……Gary Fotherby is here because he knocked Melanie's husband off his bike, and Gerald English is here because he made flippant remarks after the event."

"But that sort of thing happens every day. Why them? And you haven't said how they got here either."

"Oh she's good…."

"Look, just stop with the sexist flattery bullshit and answer the fucking question."

He raises a cautionary eyebrow, but does as he's told.

"Melanie's daughter summoned me to mete out revenge on that particular pair of miscreants."

"Melanie's daughter…. Right. So let me get this straight, and I hope everybody else is following. If you take us all back to pre-fire 2018 then, as you said, Greg won't have his accident. Melanie's daughter, Emma? Is that right? Emma wouldn't have any reason to contact you, would she? No! Don't interrupt! And if you take us back to 1991, well who knows? Melanie might never even have a daughter."

The demon delivered a slow handclap of congratulations. I should have joined in. I was proud of her. I'm not sure if her reasoning was absolutely correct, but she always stood up to him, and got away with it.

"I'm right aren't I? This time-travel idea of yours is a load of crap. You have no intention of doing any of it, do you?"

We all looked at him. You could have heard a pin drop, at least until he smiled and shook his head. "Spot on, Mrs A. You're right. At least, I can't do 1991."

At which point the pin's contact with the ground, however loud, would have been drowned out by Melanie's scream.

"You bastard. You promised me you'd take me back. You said you would make everything right."

She is out of her chair and shaking with anger, and I imagine that only her knowledge of the probable consequences hold her back from physical assault.

"Whoa! I told you I would make things right. And I will. But I can't take you back to where you want to go."

"So what was that conversation we've just had all about? And anyway; you brought him back from the future. What's so special about James, or is that just a hoax?"

"No, that wasn't a hoax. But he's the only one I've ever actually moved through time. It's not as easy as you might think!"

I'm not sure if anyone here thought that moving people through time was easy; he's jumping to conclusions there. But I have to take issue with him, although Trisha jumps in first and does it for me.

"Hang on. You took me and Chris back to 1991, didn't you?"

"Ah yes. I was forgetting that. But there was a bit of fiction involved too. I made some of it up for effect."

Well that finally clears that one up for me, but I can't say it helps much. And Derek, for the first time since I met him, is starting to look a bit less confident. He looks like a chef in a Michelin starred restaurant who, having regaled his diners with a mouth-watering menu, serves up a cheese sandwich because he doesn't actually know how to cook. The question now is, how good is the cheese sandwich? He's still claiming he can put things right and I'm not ruling it out. Anybody who could lay claim to being a combination of Time Lord and the greatest ever set designer deserves a hearing. But he's got some explaining to do.

"So if you can't take us all back to 1991 again, for which I'm truly grateful by the way; if you can't, then why did you get us all here and have us arguing over when it should be?"

I probably sounded a bit peeved, but Trisha was furious, and once again seemed to get away with expressing her strong opinion.

"You bloody time-waster! We were enjoying a week of sight-seeing before we move house. We wanted to go for a day out on the river and instead, here we are on your blasted rattling prison, only to be told you don't really need us after all. What's wrong with you? Seems like you're just wasting our time, unless of course you can give us the morning back. That would help, unless it buggers up too many time lines for you."

He has the decency to look slightly abashed when he replies, which is an improvement on turning her into a pillar of salt, or whatever the modern demonic equivalent is.

"Sorry about that," he says, his purple light at its dullest, "although I hoped you might see the funny side….No?... But, you see, I thought I could do it. Well I can't. Not with so many of you." He sees Melanie, who appears to be too angry and upset to speak, pointing at James. "Yes, I told you. I've done it with him, and them, but that didn't really affect anybody else. But you, Trisha, sorry, sorry; Mrs Adwell; you figured it out. If I take you all back, even if it's only to 2018, then half the people on the train will disappear. It'll make the whole train practically pointless."

He finishes that little speech by folding his arms and setting his face into a stubborn pout. We humans all look at each other and then vocalise our conclusion that "It is pointless!"

But you can't keep a good demon down, although that raises a couple of interesting questions: 1. Is he good? And

2. Why can't you? He reacts almost like a mother would if we'd told her she had an ugly baby. I swear I saw little purple tears forming in his eyes. But he's angry, and suddenly, disturbing the air like a mini tornado, he's out of the door, presumably to comfort his precious engine.

"So much for saving the world. Now what do we do?"

James gets up. "I have an idea." And he follows the demon out of the door. Charlie comes out from behind his counter, walks over and places a plate at the table next to me.

"Here's the cheese sandwich you wanted, sir."

Something's Cooking

Gradually, with no sign of either the demon or James, we had no choice but to find our way back to our seats on the train. It was obvious from the looks that we received as we climbed back on board that our raised voices had been overheard. That and watching the demon stalking huffily towards his engine and Melanie slamming a carriage door in floods of tears tweaked the air of unrequited curiosity up to eleven. Again, I was glad to be a part of whatever relieved the monotony for Derek's inmates, but I wasn't about to divulge the theme of our conversation.

("What was all that about?" "Oh nothing, really. We were just trying to figure out if we could all go back in time.")

So while I didn't feel any particular animosity towards the fly-tipper, the horse killer, the dangerous driver and the keyboard warrior, at least not today, I arranged my features into their finest menacing glare and was able to force a way through to a secluded spot.

"I don't see James anywhere, do you?"

"Maybe he's doing some cooking. Isn't it supposed to be a Murder Mystery Dinner thing?"

"Of course. But last time we saw him, he was heading off to see the head honcho. Said he had an idea. I'm intrigued to know what it is."

"Me too. God. I can't believe that our little mate James has managed to, how can I put this?.... work his way into such a bizarre future."

"He was such a quiet lad too. Do you remember that time that you joked that you would take him to the south of France instead of me? He blushed crimson to the roots."

"Well he was only seventeen. Just as well we can't tell what our future's going to bring."

"Ah, well you say that. But apparently, thirty years down the line the whole lot of us are going to be in the guano. And you and I were, or so we thought, supposed to be helping his nibs to save the world. What happened to that idea? Pffft!"

"So we're back to James's idea. Shall I see if I can find him? Oh, hang on, we could ask…er….Maureen, is it?"

Because it is she, or it, or whatever, who has just popped in to see if we would like a drink and some pre-dinner nibbles. So Trisha asks,

"Have you seen James, or perhaps you call him Jimbo, anywhere? Do you know where he is?"

"I'm very sorry, dear. I haven't seen him."

"Is he not busy getting dinner ready?"

"Oh no, dear. It's me and Melanie; not that she's much

use at the moment, and Charlie from the café. Oh, and young Keeley. She's very enthusiastic about tonight's game, I don't mind telling you."

"So you don't know where he is?"

"No, dear. Look! Wine, beer, nuts? Come on! I've got loads to do. I'm trying to encourage that lot to dress for dinner."

"Any Sauvignan Blanc? Couple of glasses of that?"

"It'll be white. Definitely. And I'll bring some nuts anyway if you can't make your minds up."

I recognise that demonic quirk of being unable to have a completely polite conversation.

***

She doesn't tell us anything more helpful when she returns with two small bottles of white wine, which have come from a very anonymous vineyard via a very inefficient fridge. The labels convey the information 'Vin Blanc'. I'm not optimistic.

Maureen looks us up and down, and then leaves with a curt, "You'll do, I suppose."

"That's nice," says Trisha, "Coming from a woman who would really struggle to scrub up well."

***

Our secluded spot was one of the empty private compartments. Every now and then, curious faces would peer in at us, the faces of people who were making an effort to dress up for the evening. An assortment of elegant dresses and coquettish hats, the occasional suit with unfashionably wide lapels and too brightly coloured ties were paraded past our window. The situation that all this glamour couldn't disguise was the developing fug that we'd noticed as we'd stepped onto the train earlier. Taking over from the oily, smoky aromas one would expect to drift back from the locomotive was the odour of people trying to keep clean after a few days cooped up together in a small area, their hygiene facilities very inadequate.

We were interrupted again, but this time not by the demon lady. There was a diffident tap at the door.

"Gerald, isn't it?" I remembered after I had beckoned him in.

"That's right, sir. Afternoon, Missus. I hope you don't mind me buttin' in like. But some of us 'as been talking and we was wonderin', well, hoping, really, if you might 'ave some influence with 'im that's keeping us all stuck in this train. Juss that you seem to be friends or something."

"Friends!" Trisha almost spills her wine, which was probably the best thing you could do with it. "If I hear that word once more….."

"Definitely more of the 'or something'. But I don't think he's an easy man to influence."

"Man!" Gerald suddenly becomes very agitated, bordering on hysterical. "He's not a man! 'Avent you seen him? He's a fucking monster, pardon my French, Missus. We've got women and kiddies all trapped here and now he's threatening to 'ave one of us murdered. Juss for fun, like. I don't know how to stop him; none of us do. We just thought….we're getting desperate, man!"

"I'm sorry, mate. We don't completely understand why he's doing this. But we'll go and have a word next time the train stops."

"And that's another thing. It hardly ever stops. It's drivin' me mad. And now he's got us dressing for dinner. Dressing for me bleedin' funeral more like."

I wasn't sure if the loud checked sports jacket, pin-striped trousers and trainers were really suitable for either occasion, but I felt it would have been tactless to add criticism of this fashion statement to his list of burdens.

After he left, we decided it would be a good time to go and find Derek; see if he knew where James was. Well he would, of course. He seemed to know everything. And now we also had the passengers' grievances to work into the conversation. I was becoming a bit worried about the Murder thing. I mean more than you normally would be if you knew somebody was about to be killed. Because now, I wasn't sure if Derek was actually capable of taking the victim back in time to a point before their untimely death. Our last chat on the subject hadn't filled me with confidence. Okay, he'd managed it with James, but what was his plan? Time-travel for just the murder victim, or for everybody on the train? I'd never had cause to doubt his abilities before, but then I'd never seen him doubt them himself until our 'conference' earlier.

The train was just pulling into Princes Risborough station. As soon as it stopped we alighted, through a door that would allow the two of us to leave, but nobody else. Derek leaned out of the locomotive's cab and waved to us, his usual strange smile back in place.

"Ah! My very special guests. I hope they're looking after you back there."

"Doing their best, I think. But if we ever do this again, perhaps you could add an experienced sommelier to the crew."

Trisha glares at me and I narrowly avoid her elbow in my ribs.

"Never mind that. Honestly, Chris! We came to ask if you knew where James has got to."

And Derek raises his hand and points to somewhere behind us.

"Yes. There he is. Look."

We turn round to look, and there, on the London-bound platform, is James. But it's James without his eye-patch. He waves and then walks towards the edge of the platform; James without his slight limp.

Derek raises his other hand, and James vanishes.

"Good man, Jimbo," the demon whispers, which I barely hear over the exhalations of the engine. And then louder, to us; "It appears his mission was successful. The workman has proven to be worthy of his hire. Luke chapter ten, I think you'll find."

But we're not looking at Luke; we're trying to figure out where James has gone.

Murder Mystery Dinner

The Murder Mystery event went as well as any reasonable person would have expected; that is to say, it was a complete failure. Actually, that's a rather severe judgement, because there was a death and there was dinner. The remaining crew on the train did their best with their limited catering experience, caring for the whims of carnivores, vegetarians and children as well as they could. Jimbo had left behind a very good lasagne which was portioned up and got ready for the station's microwave. The other choices on the menu were cold baked chicken fillet with lemon and thyme or a beetroot, butternut and goat's cheese tart. The meals were all pre-packed; the skill involved was in the presentation. Melanie had hosted many a dinner party in the life she'd enjoyed before demons had become involved in it, and she was instructing Keeley in the art of putting side-salads together. Melanie was still reeling from the shock of once again being let down by the demon, resulting in the reversal of familiar norms, an enthusiastic teenager being coached by a morose tutor.

It didn't really matter how much work went into the presentation of the meal, with the after-dinner entertainment hanging over them all like a Sword of Damocles. The only person who seemed to be looking forward to it was Ginny Tucker, who had convinced herself, after her conversation with Melanie, that the whole thing was reality television at its most creative. She had been particularly selective when sorting through the bags of second-hand clothes, being very impressed with what the posh people of this part of the world throw away, and now she looked the business, like she was ready for a girls' night out. Just like on earlier girls' nights out, she was wondering what she should do with the kids. She couldn't leave them with Gaz, obviously, because he was her date for the evening and anyway he was far too mesmerised by her freshly-squeezed curves to be of any use on the childcare front. So she relented, and agreed that Maureen could take the children off somewhere after their dinner and keep them entertained, providing she could vet the stories in advance, and she would prefer it if Maureen didn't refer to them as Huey, Louie and Dewey, thanks very much.

Derek had dressed up for the evening too; his idea as host was to look like the villain from an Edwardian silent movie melodrama, a look that suggested he might take one of the women out and tie her to the railway track at any moment. Tony Barnes ventured to say as much, until his wife shushed him.

"For goodness sake, Tony! Don't go putting ideas in his head."

"It was just a joke, dear. And besides, your name wasn't on the ballot paper."

His attempt to introduce some humour into the proceedings came to a halt when he remembered that of course his name *was* on the list. Chris also attempted to alleviate the tension by engaging Tony in a very pedantic discussion about where the apostrophe should be in 'goat's cheese'.

Annabel said she wasn't bothered where it went as long as they kept the foul stuff away from her. Gerald overheard and felt free to add his two penn'orth.

"I don't think punctuation matters, mate."

"No? Try moving the decimal point on your hourly rate. See where that gets you."

Chris and Trisha's earlier conversation with Derek had left them feeling slightly less anxious about the outcome of the evening, although there's bound to be some anxiety when you know somebody in the room is going to die. Witnessing a murder would be a new experience for both of them. But Derek was brimming with confidence, presenting James to them at the Princes Risborough station like a conjurer pulling a rabbit from a hat.

"Why did you ever doubt my power?"

"I think it's mainly because you did."

***

Melanie, however, had had no such conversation, nor had she been present when James had reappeared. In fact she'd had no conversation with Derek at all. She was too angry to speak to him; could barely speak to anybody else. And he seemed to be avoiding her too. She very much doubted whether he had the capacity for a guilty conscience. Letting her stew was probably just another one of his cruel punishments..

He can't take us back in time, but everything is going to be all right! Melanie couldn't understand that. How could everything be alright? And how many more times was she going to have to put up with his piecemeal way of giving out information? She knew that part of her motivation was selfish. She thought that the demon could take her back to a point where none of her vengeful actions had started, with none of their dire consequences. But that wasn't the most important thing anymore. Greg had been severely disabled for three years now. That's what she had really believed could be changed by the demon's intervention. But now? She could kill him. *Don't suppose that's even possible.* She wondered if Maureen would know the answer to that. Probably, but it would be a difficult question to ask. She had no idea what demons thought about loyalty to their own kind.

And then something happened which changed the course of her thoughts completely. Maureen followed her as she headed to the ladies' loo on the station platform. She felt the need to freshen up before the dinner started. It was hot work in the cramped kitchen area and even with her miraculous self-refreshing uniform, there was no substitute for splashing cold water on her face. Somehow this bizarre evening had to be endured. She was just running some water into the basin when Maureen came through the door.

"Feeling the strain a bit, are you? Not your usual sunny self, I notice."

"Ha bloody ha. I can't remember the last time I felt sunny."

"Oh what a shame." Melanie wondered if this was more demon sarcasm, but when she turned to look, Maureen was standing there with her head on one side, one finger at her lips, looking, for all the world, genuinely sympathetic. But you can't tell with demons.

"Did you want something?"

"Yes. A message from our host: Tell Mrs Rainham to hang on to her toothbrush. She's going home tonight."

At first Melanie didn't respond, hardly registering what she'd heard and then almost dismissing it as a cruel joke.

"What did you say?"

"I said you're going home. You're to meet me here after the dinner thing is finished and I'm to give you a lift back. So, chop chop! You have a job to do."

***

Half an hour later, back on the stationary train, dinner was being served. The passengers had been compelled to choose something from the menu, but there wasn't a universal enthusiasm for consuming any of the food. Big Charlie had once again supplied something less exotic for Ginny's kids, so they were happy.

"There's no way I'm giving my youngest any of that beetroot tart. Her nappies are bad enough as it is."

Ginny, though, was quite keen to eat, "But I can't have too much. It took me ages to get myself into this dress. I don't want it splitting on the telly. I'd never hear the last of it"

The extended Barnes family had finally agreed to leave their private compartment, hardly big enough for six anyway, and eat with everybody else in one of the open carriages, which was this evening doubling as a dining car. The tables were decorated with small vases of flowers and napkins, and cutlery that mostly matched. Keeley had been bustling about with her new-found enthusiasm, and Melanie had transitioned from looking stunned and miserable to stunned and mystified. She still couldn't get any information from Derek, which was not at all out of character for him, infuriatingly, but just to have that bombshell dropped on her without a word of explanation! And why couldn't he tell her himself instead of sending his minion? She wondered if the Adwells knew, but she wasn't going to give them the satisfaction of raising the subject with them and then finding out that they were better informed than she was. And the demon's contact with her since he'd come back on the train? Negligible. He'd winked at her, and then turned his attention to the dinner guests

The dinner progressed with periods of uncomfortable silence and stop/start conversations. None of these people had bonded to any great extent during the few days of their forced association. The relative newbies, Chris and Trisha (Beetroot, butternut and goat's (or goats') cheese tarts) were making some headway in establishing a rapport with Phil and Dinah Barnes (Cold baked chicken fillets with extra chips left over by their daughter). Philip was determined to share the outrage of the questionnaire that his parents had been presented with and asked them what they thought of the bloody cheek of it. After a brief scan of the document, Chris thought it was hilarious and couldn't see anything ethically wrong with it. He wondered if he could get some copies made to hand out to one or two people that he knew, but he decided it was safer to just say, "Yes, well I can see why you're upset." Diplomatic and non-committal to a fault.

Eavesdropping at the next table was Gerald (two child portions of cheeseburger and chips).

"I'm just here for saying what I think. That questionnaire was an insult. And me missus and her kid ain't done nothing at all. I thought you was trying to put a good word in for us. What happened with that?"

Chris shook his head. "He's not budging, I'm afraid. Sorry."

Gerald slams a hand down on the table, making the cutlery jump and the vase fall over. Keeley (too nervous and excited for anything from the menu) is quickly on the scene to mop up the spillage, and kindly offers to replace the drink that he's just finished. He hardly seemed to notice and she backs away towards the kitchen.

"Looks like I'll have to beg then. I'm not too proud to beg," he says.

"Calm down, dear. You'll give yourself a heart attack." Bella (Cold roasted chicken fillet) has been worried about her other half's health for a while. Practically everything seems to stress him out these days, even before they came here. Finding the family in the possession of a demon really isn't helping one little bit.

In the kitchen, Keeley pours Gerald another beer and then realises that Maureen (all the leftover Cold Baked Chicken fillets) still has the little bottle of liquid that will make Gerald's beer really special. She leaves the drink on a tray and goes in search of Maureen, who is at the far end of the train with the younger children, entertaining them with a bit of shape-shifting, improvising after the young Barnes girl said that balloon animals freaked her out. Maureen pulls the little bottle out of her pouch and hands it to Keeley and then morphs from a kangaroo into a pygmy hippo, the most requested animal so far. Keeley returns to the kitchen, amused that you never can anticipate what Maureen will do next, but then is dismayed to discover that the beer has gone. Her first reaction is to curse Melanie (red wine and a cracker) for being so efficient, but then thinks that if Gerald follows his usual pattern, there will be plenty more beers to doctor.

And that's when all hell breaks loose in the dining area; the crash of glass, plates and cutlery landing on the floor, the thud of a heavy body landing with them, a woman's scream, which Keeley recognised as coming from her mother. There was no doctor in the house, but somebody had to ask anyway. The mixture of generally alarmed noises contained the advice to 'give him air' and 'loosen his tie'. When Keeley rushed back into the room, she saw the prone form of Gerald, clutching his chest, his face turning a very unhealthy colour and her mother flapping about in great distress. Bella looked at the demon, and shouted,

"Can't you do something? Instead of just standing there smiling?"

Derek was indeed displaying his irritating half smile. He looked at Keeley and gave her a discreet nod before answering.

"I have no intention of doing anything. I did say that there was going to be a death this evening, if you recall. Surely you remember? Murder Mystery Evening? Yes? And I think, if somebody would like to check, the unfortunate Gerald has left us. Mrs Rainham. You do it."

Oh great! Another shitty job. I'm really earning my freedom here. Melanie confirms that she can't find a pulse and Bella starts wailing in earnest. Trisha goes over to try and console her, as Bella's daughter is noticeably reticent in providing comfort for her mum.

"Excellent!" The demon claps his hands to get attention. "So, ladies and gentlemen; we have our murder victim. Now it's up to you to figure out who did it. I've prepared these check sheets….." He reaches into his cloak and produces several sheets of paper, but his audience is unreceptive to say the least.

"Are you completely mental?" shouts Philip Barnes. "We've just had a bloke drop dead in front of us, and you expect us to play fucking Cluedo! It ain't happening! We need to call the police."

"There's no signal." says young Charlie, wide-eyed but informative.

"Then you need to let somebody leave to get help."

"Help?" The demon is starting to look annoyed. "We don't need any help. Mr English here is beyond help anyway. Look! I've had this event planned all week. Don't go spoiling it all."

Chris shakes his head. Even though he has insider's knowledge of the demon's unique way of putting things right in the end, he recognises that this supernatural creature still has volumes to learn about human nature. Tony Barnes steps forward.

"And we've been telling you all week that we don't want to play your ridiculous game. None of us wanted to die, and none of us wanted to kill anybody either. And look what you've done to this poor lady and her little girl."

The little girl in question, Keeley, smirked at being so described, but then returned to her current default expression of confusion, wondering why he'd died when she hadn't had the opportunity to poison his beer.

The demon replies testily: "Well you say that, but the late Mr English came top of the poll and somebody volunteered to carry out the coup de gras. And 'this poor lady', as you describe her, was one of the ones who voted for him."

"What? I did no such thing. Why would I want him dead? I know he has a big mouth and could get up people's noses, but he wouldn't hurt a fly. He did his best to look after us. He has a heart of gold underneath it all."

"Had."

"What are you on about?"

"You said 'he has a big mouth, has a heart of….."

"Oh shut up, you evil bastard. We've had enough of your games."

"Fine, Mr Barnes! And the rest of you? Not playing? Very well. But remember this. One of you is a murderer. I'm going to look at my engine." It seems a pity to waste the opportunity for melodrama, so he doesn't, and in a whirl of white smoke, his purple eyes glowing like never before, he wraps his cloak around himself and makes for the door, and he would have made it if Keeley hadn't stopped him.

"Um…could I have a word?"

Doorstep Challenge

The passengers decided, in the interests of decency, that Gerald's body should be carried off the train and laid somewhere quiet; showing respect to somebody they hadn't really respected much when he was alive. His widow didn't seem a bad sort though, and the effort that went into supporting her in her grief helped to distract from the shock that everybody felt at having somebody murdered, poisoned being the general speculation, right before their eyes.

Gary and Darryl are appointed to carry the deceased from the train, being the youngest and strongest of the men. They leave him covered up in the shop, just for the night, until they can figure out what to do with him, or what they'll have permission to do with him. As Gary climbs back onto the train, Ginny takes him by the arm and says, quietly,

"I thought the acting was brilliant. Is he alright now?"

Gary looks at her as if he's seeing something for the first time.

"Course he's not alright, you fuckwit. He's dead. Jesus!"

Ginny hardly falters, "Oh, well that's sad, but it'll be good for the ratings."

***

Melanie, concluding that dinner and the show are definitely over, tables are cleared, washing-up's done, goes in search of Maureen, as requested. She finds her out on the platform, talking to Derek. *At flippin' last. Maybe I'll get some answers.*

"Ah Mrs Rainham! Are you ready to go? Maureen is going to give you a lift home."

"Of course I'm ready. I've been ready all week. But I don't understand what's going on. What's changed? I thought you said you couldn't take me back in time."

"No. Well actually, yes and no. What I said was that I couldn't take so many people back in time. And you're not going back in time. You're going home now, in, what is it? 2022 by your calendar? I'm sure you're keen to see everybody again."

"Of course I am. But how does that help Greg? You told me you were going to put things right. His accident was three years ago….."

Derek holds up his hand to stop her.

"I don't know! Do you want the zip treatment again? You really are the most demanding so-and-so. You were the one that got me involved in the first place. I've spent considerable amounts of my precious time and energy doing your bidding, and still it's not enough for you."

"Now just a minute! Whose idea was it for me to work my backside off serving drinks to your latest bunch of victims? I did my best with that, and you said you'd picked a good point in time for me to go back to."

"Well I have….. And it's now. That's the best time. So off you go. Maureen will take you in the van. Don't forget your seatbelt; I understand she drives like Jehu."

"Jehu?"

"Oh dear. I forget you modern suburbanites know virtually nothing about the Bible. Second book of Kings, chapter nine, verse twenty, if you can be bothered to look it up. He'd have loved Gary's van."

"That again! But you told me that if I go back now I'll be facing a police investigation."

"Look! I'm not going to change the whole world so it fits in with the way you want to go. I'm sure you and your husband will figure something out. Maybe you can pretend to be his new girlfriend. That's an idea! I could do you some documents if you like!"

Melanie thinks that probably just getting away from this supernatural bane of her life as quickly as possible and dealing with any consequences in the good old human way might be her best course of action right now.

"No. It's okay. I'll figure something out."

"Off you go then. Thanks for your help. And I'm so sorry that you never got round to spilling tea on Gary, but I'll be thinking of you next time I do it."

At the end of a twenty minute white-knuckle ride, Melanie has the first glimpse of her home. The hedges have grown a bit, but are still very neatly trimmed. Greg was always very particular about the look of them; perhaps he has somebody come to do it for him now. There's a different car on the drive, unsurprising after four years, and Greg would need something adapted to suit his disability.

"I can see you're nervous, dear. I expect things will sort themselves out, but how about we do a quick change on your clothes …...like that. There'll be enough to talk about without having to explain the uniform."

Melanie looks down and wonders if Greg will remember that these were the clothes she was wearing when she left four years ago. She opens the door and steps out onto the pavement, and the van speeds away with a squeal of tyres. A curtain twitches, letting out a wash of light from the living room, but it's almost dark outside and whoever moved the curtain could probably only see the tail-lights of the van as it sped away. She walks, trembling now, towards the front door. She senses that there's something not quite right about what she's seeing, but is too focused on her next encounter to think about what it is.

She almost trips up the three steps leading to the door, then steadies herself to stand nervously on the doorstep; the automatic porch light means she can no longer hide. This is what she wanted, isn't it? So she reaches up with a shaky finger and rings the bell. Still the annoying Westminster Chimes. And the three steps…

She sees a tall figure advancing towards her, just a dark shape through the frosted glass of the door. The door opens wide, and Greg is standing there, as tall as he ever was. They look at each other in stunned silence for a couple of seconds, and then Melanie collapses, not exactly into his arms, but the ex-rugby player still has enough of his reaction speed to catch her before she hits the ground.

Sits Vac

Trisha and I watched in disbelief at the debacle that was supposed to be the Murder Mystery Evening. I had every confidence that things would be put right in the end, just as the demon had said, but in the meantime, his understanding of human nature was proving to be pretty patchy. Did he really think that these people were now going to sit down and play some sort of a quiz? (Tell me, Mr A; what was your relationship to the deceased?)

No. They were horrified, angry, revolted, grief-stricken and powerless. Whatever anti-social misdemeanours they may have committed to earn themselves a ticket on this train, I didn't think they deserved all this. The demon's response to their expressions of outrage was to look more and more annoyed; offended that they had spoiled his game, and so he went off in a huff, albeit with a spectacularly smoky exit.

"What are we supposed to do now?" Trisha muttered to me, exactly the question I'd been about to ask her. I shook my head, a head devoid of ideas. So she suggested that I should follow him, try to reason with him.

"Why me?"

"He's your bloody demon, isn't he?"

I'll admit we've had some history, but I wasn't happy with the suggestion that I possessed a demon. Nevertheless, it seemed like a good idea, and it would be a relief to get away from all the noise and pandemonium in the train, but before I could make a move, Melanie opened the door and left. I attempted to follow, but the door had locked again. I decided to go in search of other exits, but they were all locked. So once again we were being controlled, our freedom rationed.

***

Trisha is really angry and is in mid-rant, when the door opens and our host, whose charm is wearing very thin with me, and everybody else I would guess, enters the carriage. He holds up his hand for silence, and gets it. His audience is familiar with the cost of disobedience. He looks peeved, like a company accountant about to deliver the inadequate quarterly trading results to a group of under-performing junior executives.

"I have to say, ladies and gentlemen, that this has been a very disappointing evening, and I want you to share my pain."

The very distressed Bella can't let this go.

"Your pain? You've had my Gerald killed, you monster. Don't talk to me about pain."

"Ah yes. About that. I had indeed intended for that to happen. After all, he did receive the most votes. But it turns out that he wasn't murdered."

"What? We've just carried his body out."

"And I thank you for that, Mr Clark. But it turns out that he died of a cardiac arrest. So as I say, a very disappointing evening. No murder and hardly any of you ate your dinners. I hate to see food being wasted."

Normally I'd be right with him on that one, but his inhuman lack of tact and compassion overrode any shortcomings in their appreciation for the cuisine. I suppose he can't entirely help being inhuman, given who he is. Tony Barnes dares to speak up.

"Hang on a moment. You're saying that there was a willing murderer, but that they didn't go through with it. So who was it?"

"I see, Mr Barnes. So now you want to spoil the 'Mystery' part of the evening too."

"We don't care about your stupid game. Don't you get it? I don't think anybody's in the mood for a round of twenty questions; am I right?"

I got the impression that he was right. The whole party looked as if they could have advanced with pitchforks and torches at that moment. Definitely a castle-burning vibe going round.

"Very well. As much as I resent being harried by a group of social reprobates," (*See what I mean about tact?*), "I pride myself in being a being of my word. I promised the person that put themselves forward to be murderer that they and their family could go home. It is perhaps unfortunate that one of the family has already left us; the late Mr English."

Well that went down well. There was a collective gasp from the room, but Bella was quick enough to realise that her daughter was the guilty party; process of elimination, really. She knew she hadn't volunteered, and Keeley was the only one who hadn't joined in with the gasping. Instead, she glared back at her mother with a face that showed not a hint of remorse.

"What have you done, Keeley?"

"Nothing, Mother, it turns out. More's the pity."

"But how could you even think of doing something like that? I know he wasn't perfect, but I loved him. And he's spent years looking after you."

"Years picking on me and criticising me, more like. I can't figure out what you ever saw in him, the fat bastard. It's no wonder he had a heart attack."

Bella burst into tears again. I couldn't say I blamed her. A bereavement and a hideous discovery about your only child in the space of an hour is a lot to take. Keeley had pushed her way past the riveted audience and fled down the corridor. I thought about the demon's promise to allow the murderer and family to go home. What a happy home that was going to be. I looked up at Derek, still in his Edwardian villain's outfit, and wondered what trick he had up his capacious sleeve, because, judging by the half-grin, there was going to be something. He was reliably devious.

I was also puzzled about the two noticeable absentees from the party, James, gone on some mission, and now Melanie. There was something going on, and now Derek was back on board, I could ask him.

"What's going on?" I asked him; not the most incisive question, I admit, but it covered all the main points and he

251

seemed to divine my meaning. I hadn't yet spotted the silver lining attached to the clouds that had gathered in his prison train. The miscarriages of justice more like! Good one. I must remember that for my memoirs.

"Chris! I'm sorry we haven't had much time to chat this evening. Such a lot going on, isn't there? And so much fuss and noise."

"I think you've upset a lot of people this evening."

"Really? But they can't see the bigger picture like you and I, can they?" Coming from him, this bordered on a compliment, but my version of the bigger picture was just a frame and a canvas with a few brush strokes. I could do with a bit more detail.

At this point, Trisha came back from the far end of the train to report on 'the most godawful row' going on between Bella and her daughter, although that was hardly surprising.

"But the thing is," said Trisha, "the girl says she doesn't want to go home."

The demon brightens at hearing this bit of news.

"Splendid! Because I need a new trolley dolly."

"Trolley dolly?"

"She's a bit young to be Head of Customer Services yet. But her prospects are good…..What?"

"What's happened to Melanie, for goodness sake?" I always find the prospects of having a straightforward conversation with him are not good.

"Did I not say? I've sent her home. Mo's taken her in the van."

"What do you mean, 'home'?"

"Oh come on, Chris. Surely even you know what a home is. Haven't you just bought a new one?"

That's his earlier compliment cancelled out then.

"And it's such a nuisance. I lose my chef and my Head of Customer Services on the same day. I don't suppose either of you…..? No. You want to go home too, am I right?"

"Yes we do. But I have to ask; exactly how are you going to put everything right again? It all looks like chaos, if you ask me."

"Oh, that! It's all done. I'll be more than happy to tell you about it. But I could do with a cup of tea. Let's go to Charlie's."

So we did, and he told us his simple but effective method for saving the world.

***

The demon's explanation, which left us stunned at its ingenuity, concluded with, "So if you should look him up in Oxford, don't mention any of this to him. He's only twenty-one and he won't have a clue what you're talking about."

The explanation included the information that James had 'gone home' to 2050, a much happier man. I reflected that, given my age now, there was a fair to middling chance that I might not live long enough to meet the 2050 version of James, much to my regret. Perhaps if I cut down my weekly alcohol units…….

Alright For Some

James Reese was taking a trip down Memory Lane, or more accurately, Oxford High Street. It was the autumn of 2018 and James hadn't been here for over thirty years, but some things never changed, and the beautiful architecture that makes up the various universities was still the same in 2050.

Today, though, he's not here to admire the scenery. As he said to Melanie on the train, he's here to find himself, or again, more accurately, deliver a note to his younger self. He knows that this is the day of Kim's watery accident and his own quick thinking rescue.

As he stands looking down from Magdalen Bridge he sees three figures in the boat that he once was in; Kim and two other students whose names he can't quite recall now. But his younger self is not on board. He sees Kim standing up and fooling around, but turns away at the sound of the splash and ensuing commotion. He doesn't need to see Kim drown. And then he discovers he doesn't need the eye-patch anymore. He realises that the future, both for him personally and globally, has been changed.

The note he left for himself at the university porter's lodge read:

Kim's been shagging your girlfriend.

Later, much later; the following year in fact, James enters the small supermarket at The Plain roundabout. He looks up to find something, it doesn't matter what, on one of the high shelves, so high in fact, that he can't reach it. He turns and politely asks a tall, blonde woman in a green coat who is about to leave the shop if she would mind reaching the object for him. She smiles and says of course she can do that. As she reaches up, there is the sound of an altercation from the road outside. A cyclist and a truck driver are squaring up to each other, noisy accusations of poor driving standards being shouted. It soon fizzles out, as these things do, only to lead to arguments and abusive comments much later on Facebook.

***

"You look disgustingly smug, I have to say, Derek."

"You didn't have to say it, but I think I have good reason to be. Although the wording on the note was James's idea. He clearly was the best person to know how to upset himself."

***

Trisha is looking impatient, less inclined to join in the back-slapping and congratulations than I am.

"Very impressive, and if I wasn't so tired I'm sure I would appreciate it more. Perhaps in the privacy of our own home would be nice.. Can we go now? You obviously don't need us here."

"Of course. I think you'll find your car can be unlocked now. Good luck, and of course, if you ever need me…."

"We won't!" And she fishes the keys from her pocket, keen to get away. I hesitate for a moment.

"What about Melanie? She's still presumably a suspected arsonist."

"What about her? There's a very good chance you might never see her again. You're moving away. Were you planning to call the police again? I can't see her husband turning her in, can you? If they're clever enough, she could get away with it. The heat's died down, as it were."

"I'd better catch up with Trisha, I suppose."

"You'd better. I don't think she's warmed to me quite the way you have, has she?"

I thought 'warmed to me' was possibly exaggerating how I felt, but I shook his hand anyway.

"Goodbye…er…Derek."

"Au revoir?"

"Yeah, probably."

"Good job she didn't hear that, eh!"

Back in the car I breathed a heavy sigh as Trisha turned the ignition key. We both waved as Maureen came careering back into the car park in the white van, and Trisha put the car into gear and left before she could be subjected to any more demonic nonsense.

"So what's on your list for tomorrow, love?"

***

257

Maureen had one more important trip in Gary's van. She had to take Bella back home, as promised. They decided to wait until daylight as Bella, exhausted from crying and arguing, hadn't fallen asleep until the early hours of the morning. So Maureen and Derek took advantage of the time off to go and have a lie down and do whatever it is that demons do when they're in bed together.

("I hope you're taking precautions!" "Of course I am; there's a fire extinguisher in the corner.")

Afterwards, as Derek lies there, strumming his newly acquired Gibson Les Paul, he confesses,

"I must admit, I'm getting a little bored with this railway line. I feel like I need something different. Or to go somewhere different."

"Any idea where?" Maureen is absent-mindedly plucking a chicken ("He loves me, he loves me not") and the chicken looks furious.

"I have an idea."

***

The still tearful Bella straps herself into the van for the ride home. She's stressing about what will happen to Gerald's body, but she's told, not to worry; it will be taken care of. And Keeley will be well taken care of too, and she's welcome to come and visit, but that particular outcome is a bit too much to take in at the moment.

Maureen makes her customary rapid progress through the country to the housing estate on the edge of Wallingford, to the small house that Bella used to share with Gerald. Maureen's unfailingly accurate internal sat-nav takes them right to the door.

"I won't come in, dear. I'm sure you can manage without me." And Bella finds herself deposited on the pavement. All seems exactly as she left it just…just when, exactly?…. apart from the large pile of fabric that somebody has dumped on her doorstep. And then the fabric moves and groans.

"Bella? Is that you? What am I doing out here?"

"Gerald? But…."

"I'm sorry, Pet. I must of had one too many last night. It won't happen again, I swear. But I've had the weirdest dreams. Something to do with a train…"

But Bella doesn't care. She's hugging Gerald with an intensity that he hasn't been used to for years.

Light At The End Of The Tunnel

After Bella's departure, the remaining passengers are feeling despondent and pessimistic. It was as if an invitation had gone out to come to a Winnie the Pooh themed party, and everybody had decided to turn up as Eeyore. The usually enthusiastic Ginny is even beginning to think that there are better things she could do with her time and wonders what she has to do to get herself voted off the show. Keeley's exuberance at hearing about the prospect of being fast tracked towards the Head of Customer Services position is insufficiently contagious to lift the mood.

"That girl's in Cloud Cuckoo Land!"

"Probably, Darryl, but she's got our Charlie clearing tables and washing-up. He would never do that at home!"

This is one of very few bright sides and, once again, the Barnses, father and son, lead the delegation of complainants. They're surprised to hear that the demon agrees with them; he's fed up with the place too.

"So will you let us leave?"

"I didn't say that. Mr Clark! Your shovelling shoulders please. This way!"

"Not again. I'm sick of this. I seem to spend most of my days covered in coal dust," Darryl complained. "I hate being dirty all the time."

"We're all sick of it," his wife joined in. "I've memorised the colours of every tee-shirt and pair of pants on every washing line on the way out of Chinnor. I can see them in my sleep! If we do much more of this I am going to literally explode."

"Oh I very much doubt that. I mean, unless you want to, obviously. I'm sure I can help with that. But it sounds like you would all benefit from a change of scenery, yes?"

Philip Barnes argues strongly that they would all benefit from getting the hell out of his stupid train and going home.

"But it's been less than a week. In your case, Mr Barnes, much less. So I'm going to give you all a little treat to break the monotony. Come along, Mr Clark!"

The long-suffering Mr Clark rolled his eyes and did as he was told, and very soon, after a brief spell of hissing and huffing, the hard-worked little locomotive got them all moving again.

"Same old, same old," muttered young Charlie, staring at the rural landscape with a twelve year old's lack of enthusiasm. The train picked up a little speed heading towards the Bledlow cricket ground, and then everything went dark as they disappeared into a tunnel.

The usual reaction when all the lights suddenly go out is for people to start screaming, and that's what happened; a blend of pitches from bass to soprano, depending on age and gender. Through the darkness came two pinpoints of purple light; Maureen's eyes glowing as she came through from the kitchen area to switch on the lights.

"Sorry about that," she says, wiping her lips, "I was just finishing my breakfast. Forgot all about the tunnel."

The screaming has abated somewhat. Children are whimpering; one of the toddlers is still wailing because Gary has tripped over her in the dark, but most of the passengers are looking in disbelief and horror at the total darkness outside the glass.

"But there isn't a tunnel on this line. Never has been. Where on earth are you taking us?"

"Wait and see, Mr Barnes. You were promised a change of scenery, aaaand, here it comes." Not scenery, as such, but now the tunnel walls at least have lights. And there's another change.

"We're climbing, aren't we?"

Gary was the first to notice this, as he struggled to his feet and then was almost overbalanced by the altered angle of the train as he picked up his daughter and passed the struggling child back to her mother. But then other people started to grip the seat backs as they felt the dual effects of incline and gravity.

"I demand to know where you're taking us!"

"Yes, Tony, dear. I thought that you, of all people, would. I think you'll have to wait till the driver has a chance to speak to you. It was his idea, not mine. I was quite happy with Chinnor, believe it or not."

"And how come we're moving uphill? The train's not making any noise."

"Ask the boss. I'm busy."

"Doing what?"

"Knitting, if you must know."

So she leaves them with no alternative but to wait and see what their host has in store for them. Gradually, the train comes to a halt, and daylight, rather than electric light, comes in through the windows. After a minute or two the door opens and the demon climbs in, looking gleeful, followed by Darryl, who looks like he's been through a very testing experience, and not just a tunnel.

"Good morning, ladies and gentlemen. You all wanted a change of scenery. Come and look at this, through these windows. Here's a scene you'll never forget."

Those of the passengers who dared to do as he said were astonished to find themselves almost three thousand metres up inside the Eiger mountain, gazing out across the Swiss Alps from the old Eigerwand Station.

"It's nothing like the Chilterns, is it? And this is a rare privilege, I can tell you. Trains haven't stopped here since 2016."

"Privilege? You call this a privilege? We wanted to go home. You are insane! Taking us from Chinnor to Switzerland is a dreadful idea. Completely idiotic! How the hell are we going to get home from here? Who's going to feed my animals now?"

"And our tropical fish?"

"Don't worry about that. It's still Monday, remember."

"And how have you got this old train up here anyway?"

"I'll admit, a few mechanical modifications were necessary. And I had to rely on my own power source. But Mr Clark was very grateful when I said he could stop shovelling coal, weren't you, lad?"

He nodded. He was grateful. But Tony Barnes, not so much.

"Let me get this straight. We're actually in Switzerland?"

"Yes, we are."

"Why?"

"Because it's the first chance I've had to get back since they started digging the tunnel. I asked Adolf if he needed my help. I have some experience working underground, you see. But he said that if I just kept sending him men with picks and shovels, that would be enough, so I left him to it. I did suggest he might try keeping them happy with bottles of red wine, but he didn't want to waste the money on them. Worked some of them to death he did."

"Adolf?"

"Oh no. Not that Adolf. Not *the* Adolf. A different one. I have to say, they made a great job of it. But wait till you see the view from the top."

As usual, he didn't really give them much choice, so they all piled back into the train and waited to see the view from the top, which turned out, after a short but bracing walk, to be a vista of snow and rock as far as the eye could see, spectacular enough to take away what little breath they had left after the climb. So there they were, this group of Britain's most reluctant tourists, dressed for the south of England in early summer, and their thoughts summed up in a nutshell by young Charlie Clark, his young lungs the first to recover.

"It's freezing."

Maureen came up behind the shivering party, ever helpful, carrying her capacious shopping bag.

"Woolly hat, anyone?"

Epilogue

The Jungfrau Railway (Jungfraubahn) in Switzerland, takes passengers through the Eiger and Munch mountains to the highest railway station in Europe. Building of this rack railway, under the guidance of Adolf Guyer-Zeller, started in 1896 and it took sixteen years to tunnel through the mountains. Accidental deaths and the subsequent industrial unrest and withdrawal of labour slowed the process. Guyer-Zeller died of a heart attack only three years into the construction.

There's no way that a steam train from Chinnor, measuring almost one and a half metres between its wheels, would fit on the Jungfraubahn's one metre track, not, as Derek said, without some mechanical modification. Nor could it climb the gradient under its own power.

But you've all seen what an enthusiastic demon can do.

What readers said about Guilt Edged

"If you often spend sleepless nights, then this is the book for you. Jolly good read in the small hours, with a tinge of black humour thrown into the mix."

Pauline Verbe, Oxfordshire

"Thoroughly good and satisfying read. If you are looking for an imaginative and intriguing plot that draws you in and grips you, I recommend this highly."

Sacha Mogg, Watlington

"Kafkaesque"

Malcolm, Watlington

"Perplexed and riveted. Loved it".

Lee Jones, Warpsgrove

"Loved it"

Jon Bradley, Watlington

"Not enough hyphens"

Jim Stubbs, Watlington

Printed in Great Britain
by Amazon

23132047R00155